# New TOEIC Listening S

U0097864

**PART 1**

*empty*
(adj) ① 空的 The streets were almost empty.
② 沒有, 缺少 His words are empty of sincerity.
他的話沒有誠意

1. ( B ) (A) The market is closed. ③ 無意義的
擁擠的 (B) The market is crowded. /kraudɪd/ 誘等的 He didn't want
骯髒的 (C) The market is dirty. to retire and lead
adj 空曠的 (D) The market is empty. an empty life.

④空虚的 It's an empty promise. (v) 使成為空的

2. ( C ) (A) The man is at the beach. He emptied out all his pockets
(B) The woman is at home. onto the table.
(C) The man is on a bicycle. 他把口袋的東西都拿出來放桌上
(D) The woman is on the sidewalk. They emptied the bottle of
把XO喝完了          XO.

The position of secretary is         ² pavement        sidewalk artist
           void.        在人行道上   = by way        路邊畫家
3. ( B ) (A) The café is full.         = footpath     sidewalk tax
(B) The café is empty. void         = walkway      給行乞者的
(C) The library is busy. = vacant                  a beggar
(D) The school is closed. = unoccupied            a vagrant
                     = available                  e ?

4. ( B ) (A) The men are fighting.
event   (B) The women are seated.   當坐下v.用時    seat → 被動 be seated
事件, 比賽項目 (C) They are eating dinner. sit → 主動 sit down
a chain of (D) This is a private event.
一連串的新事件 a course of events 事的  I seated my guests around the table.

5. ( C ) (A) This is a new building. 競 seat ⑪ 座位 Excuse me,
The teacher (B) This is the site of a funeral. 葬禮 is the seat taken?
outlined (C) This is an ancient landmark.  It was quite
landmarks (D) This is a museum. 地標, 重大事件 an event.
in the history of mankind. 師概述了人類史的  場面真夠壯觀的

6. ( D ) (A) They are factory workers. 里 It's a track and field
observatory (B) They are a dance group. 程 event. 田徑賽
⑪ (C) The restaurant is empty. 碑 看到陌生人在店附近閒晃
天文台 (D) They are students in a classroom.
觀測所 *observe He observed a stranger hanging around the store.
慶祝(節日), 遵守, 評論 看到. 觀察 The law must be strictly observed. 這項法律需要嚴格遵守
He observed that it was a lovely day. 他說天氣真好
Some people observe Christmas here.

# PART 2

7. ( A ) Did you hear that? 你有聽到嗎？
   - (A) I didn't hear anything. 我什麼都沒聽到
   - (B) I've been here for an hour. 我已在這一小時了
   - (C) That is neither here nor there. 不在這也不在那兒 ⑪ 垃圾場 = wasteyard

椅子可以丟了.
The chair is about ready
for the dump.
= junk-field
→ dump the garbage
→ You'll be fined if you
dump here. 在這倒垃圾會

8. ( B ) What's keeping Elaine? 是什麼耽擱了Elaine?
   - (A) Dump her. 甩掉他  *dump(v) 傾倒.拋棄
   - (B) She's on the phone with a client. 她在和客戶講電話
   - (C) I doubt you can keep it up. 我懷疑你能一直保持(我不覺得你可以一直保持

懷疑 不相信 不能肯定
/daut/   keep up

9. ( B ) Does your teacher speak Chinese in class? 你的老師在課堂上講中文嗎  →保持(同一速度或水準)
   - (A) Not only.
   - (B) Never.
   - (C) Few.

不止 從未 很少

繼續.保存.不下跌(精神或價格)
These props will keep up the house.
這些柱子可以把這座房子撐住

10. ( B ) Did anyone remember to call Mr. Edwards? 有人記得打電話給Edward嗎?
    - (A) Mr. Edwards is on the phone. 他在線上
    - (B) I left a message this morning. 我今早有留訊息
    - (C) Only if I remember. 只要我記得.

* finish line ←→ starting line
dead line
= due date

11. ( A ) Can I borrow ten dollars? 我可以借10元嗎?  抱歉,我身上沒有現金
    - (A) Sorry, I don't have any cash on me.
    - (B) It costs ten dollars. 花10元
    - (C) I'm willing to pay five hundred dollars. 我願意花500元

*due (adj) 應付的.欠的
That money is due to me,
but I haven't got it yet.
②正當的.合適的
He handled it with
due care.

12. ( A ) I'm never going to finish the project on time. 我一定不可能把案子準時完成
    - (A) Is there anything I can do to help? 我可以做任何事幫忙嗎?
    - (B) Did you make it to the finish line? 你有做到最後嗎?
    - (C) You're a quitter. 你是個輕易放棄 有達到終點線嗎?

②到期的
The bank loan is due
this month.
預期的
We are due to leave
tomorrow.

13. ( B ) Are they leaving so soon? 他們那麼快就要走囉?
    - (A) I'll be right back. 我很快就回來了
    - (B) Yes, I'm afraid so. 恐怕是的
    - (C) I'm wearing pants. 我有穿褲子

工作(職務)同人
(n.)① 應得之物
She asked no more
than her due. 沒有提出非分的要求

14. ( A ) How many copies of the form do you need? 你需要幾張表格副本?
    - (A) Only one. 只要一張
    - (B) Make copies of the form. 表格要複印
    - (C) The copier is out of order. 印表機壞掉了

② 應付款
I've already paid my membership dues.

GO ON TO THE NEXT PAGE.

15. ( A ) Why are you carrying an umbrella? 你為何要帶雨傘?
期望 (A) It's supposed to rain this afternoon. 今天下午應該要下雨的.
認為必須 (B) I've been carrying you for months. 我已經扶持,資助你好幾個月了
認為應該 (C) Don't open it in the house. 不要在屋裡打開  *chubby adj. 圓胖的

Marlene禮拜五都會帶甜甜圈來嗎? /do,nʌt/
16. ( B ) Does Marlene always bring doughnuts on Fridays? /tʃʌbɪ/
diet (A) That's why you're getting chubby. 那就是為何你變胖 plump 豐滿的
/'daɪət/ (B) Like clockwork. =Like a clock. 規律地 voluptuous
n.飲食,食物 (C) No, I'm on a diet. 不,我在節食 /və'lʌptʃuəs/
在減肥

17. ( C ) Didn't you use to work at McDonald's? 你以前不是在麥當勞上班嗎?
大麥克 (A) Would you like fries with that? 你想要薯條 stout adj.矮胖的
超好吃← (B) The Big Mac is very tasty. → 搭配嗎? /staut/ 結實的
(C) No, I worked at Burger King. 我在Burger King上班

那是你的表親嗎?
18. ( B ) Is that your cousin? 這齣戲是好戲 → Marathons are the real thing,
(A) The play's the thing., the real thing 真貨,好貨 these little jogs are no
(B) No, but the resemblance is striking. challenge at all.
(C) Yes, she is my sister. ↳ resemblance 了不起的經歷,成就/馬拉松賽跑才是
n. 相似 真的臺兒,慢跑狠手

你在哪裡剪頭髮的?我沒去過哈利斯堡 same 不算什麼
19. ( C ) Where did you get your haircut? /rɪ'zɛmbləns/
(A) I've never been to Harrisburg. ㄆㄧㄛ
我漸漸開始 (B) I started losing it. The children have a great resemblance
損失了 (C) At a barbershop in the mall. to their parents. 孩子們和父母十分相像.
商場裡的理髮廳 barber pole *striking adj.惹人注目的,敲擊的
His striking good looks and charm
20. ( C ) Do you know if Nelson is in town? made him very popular.
Nelson (A) The town is famous for its barbeque. 這鎮因為BBQ而有名
有在這裡嗎 (B) He said he would. 他說他會.
(C) I think he arrives this afternoon. 我覺得今天下午他會到/他已就任新職

新的軟體安裝了嗎? *install v.安裝設備,任命,使就職 He has been installed
21. ( B ) Has the new software program been installed? in his new office.
我不知道, (A) Get with the program. → To confirm or fall in line with what is expected.
問資訊部 (B) I don't know. Ask somebody in IT. No one leaves their dirty laundry in the
(C) Read the manual. 看手冊 hallway - get with the program.
IT: Information Technology guidebook, directory If you don't get with the program soon,
22. ( A ) Do you know if we have to work overtime? you're going to be off the team.
我覺得要哦 (A) I think we do. 你覺得我們要加班嗎?
(B) We get paid overtime. 我們有加班費 ②to accept new ideas and give more
work (C) I went to work. 我去上班了 attention to what is happening now
n.工作 → They have been playing the same old
v.起作用 Your suggestion works well. music for ten years now - it's time to get with
行得通 你的建議很有效 the programme.

50

23. ( C ) Do you like living in New York? 你喜歡住在紐約嗎？ ＊sometimes 偶然.有時.時常
　　(A) I've moved many times. 我已經搬過很多次家了 ＝occasionally ＝at times
　　(B) No, I live in New York. 不，我住在紐約 ＝on occasion ＝from time to time
　　(C) Sometimes. 有時候喜

你最喜歡的菜餚是什麼？ /kwɪˈzin/ 私房菜 ＊private home cuisine / deprivation cuisine
24. ( C ) What's your favorite kind of cuisine? away 個人 輕食
　　(A) Desert. 點心(正餐後的甜點) ＊snack平時小點心 /deprɪˈveʃən/
　　(B) A sports car. 跑車 The professor asked Peter to write 剝奪.免職.損失
　　(C) Italian. 義式菜色 a resume about this book. 要求彼得寫這本 deprive

你開始寄履歷了嗎？ /ˈrɛzjume/ 簡歷 書的摘要 /dɪˈpraɪv/
25. ( C ) Have you started sending out your resume? 摘要 → He was deprived of his rights.
　　(A) Work hard, play hard. 用力工作.用力玩
　　(B) Yes, I was able to fake it. 我可以裝出來.我 他被剝奪了權利
　　(C) I've sent it to a couple of firms.

你的辦公室在哪兒？ 我已經寄給幾間公司了
26. ( B ) Where is your office located? adj: 穩固的.結實的 (n.) 公司.商行
地點← (A) Yes, I've been working a lot. I don't think the chair is firm enough
　　(B) One-eleven Main Street. to stand on.
　　(C) Come to my office.
② 堅定的.堅決的 / 堅信洗冷水澡有益健康
你認識 Daniel 多久了？ My brother has a firm belief in the virtue of
27. ( B ) How long have you known Daniel? cold baths.
　　(A) He's too short. 他太矮了
　　(B) We've known each other since high school. 高中就認識彼此了
　　(C) His name is Daniel. { since+某個時間
　　　　　　　　　　　　　　 { for +一段時間

28. ( C ) Tom, this is my friend, Gary. ＊see eye to eye (與某人看法一致)
　　(A) I don't know. ＊have an eye to 照看.留意.提防
　　(B) Look at it. → He always has an eye to business. 總找機會做壞
　　(C) We've met. → Have an eye to when the gas runs out. 留意煤氣何時用完

29. ( A ) It's Fred's birthday tomorrow. ＊with an eye to 考慮到.注意到
remind to (A) Thanks for reminding me. I need to buy him a gift. We should make the plan
提醒去做 (B) Not this year. 今年不是，今年沒有 with an eye to the future.
remind of (C) We never did see eye to eye. 我們的看法沒有一致過 擬計畫時應想到未來
使想起.使記起 I can't see eye to eye with him. 我不同意他的看法
30. ( C ) How much did you pay for the tickets? ＊give an eye to → Go into the garden
piece (A) About a week. 大概一週 and give an eye to your
n. 一張.一塊 (B) I've been waiting since four. 我從四點開始等 children. 到花園裡去照看
一則消息 (C) Fifteen dollars a piece. 一塊15元 一下你的孩子們

Here is a good piece of news for you. / Could you give me a piece of paper?

GO ON TO THE NEXT PAGE.

31. ( C )  Is this your <u>coat</u>? /kot/ⓝ外套,大衣
　　　　(A) I'll have some.　層子
　　　　(B) Go get it.　a coat of paint
　　　　(C) No, that's Nancy's coat.
　　　　　ⓥ 塗在...上
　　　　　覆蓋...的表面
　　　　The pill is
藥丸包了糖衣 coated with sugar.

| | 主格 | 受格 | 所有格 | 所有代人. |
|---|---|---|---|---|
| 我 | I | me | my | mine |
| 你 | you | you | your | yours |
| 他 | he | him | his | his |
| 她 | she | her | her | hers |
| 我們 | we | us | our | ours |
| 他們 | they | them | their | theirs |
| 它 | it | it | its | X |
| | | | └→沒有 its×| |

**PART 3**

***Questions 32 through 34*** *refer to the following conversation.*

電腦斷層掃描顯示正常但是驗血結果還不確定,所以我想再多

W : The <u>CAT scan</u> appears normal but the <u>blood test</u> was <u>inconclusive</u>. So I'd like to run a few
　　more tests on you, just to be safe.　adj.非決定性的.不確.測試幾次,保險.
　　　　　　　　　　　　　　　　　　　　　定的.

M : That's fine but... what kind of tests are you talking about?
可以再測.但...你講得是哪一種測試? 第一種是核磁共振,你躺在一個巨大的圓管子裡

W : The first test is called an MRI.  You lie inside a <u>giant tube</u>, <u>sort of</u> like a tanning bed, and we
　　use lasers to <u>examine</u> your <u>entire body</u>.  It will take about an hour. 有點像助曬床,我們會用

M : That doesn't sound like fun.  I'm kind of <u>claustrophobic</u>. /klɔstrə'fobɪk/ Are you really sure I need it?
聽起來一點都不好玩 我有點幽閉恐懼症,你真的需要　　雷射機查你全身.←
　　　　　　　　　　　　　　　　　　　　　　　　　　大概會花一小時。

32. ( A )  Who are the speakers?　　　　　我做檢?
醫生和病人 (A) Doctor and patient.　adj.有耐心的
　　　　(B) Teacher and student.　　能容忍的　n.病人
　　　　(C) Husband and wife.
客人和店員 (D) Customer and clerk.　The doctor is very patient with his patients.

33. ( C )  What does the woman want to do?　　C computerized
　　　　(A) Give the man a CAT scan.　　　A axial /'æksɪəl/
量男子的溫 (B) <u>Take</u> the man's <u>temperature</u>.　T tomography /tó'magrəfɪ/
　　度 (C) Run more tests on the man.　　M magnetic /mæg'netɪk/
開一些藥 (D) <u>Prescribe</u> some medication.　R resonance /'rɛzənəns/
　　　　　└ write 開處方　　　　I imaging / 'ɪmɪdʒɪŋ/

34. ( B )  How does the man feel about taking an MRI?
興奮 (A) Excited. 做核磁共振他覺得如何?
害怕 (B) Horrified.　adj. → v. horrify 使恐懼,使反感 We were horrified by
理解 (C) Apprehensive. adj. → v. apprehend　　what we saw.
生氣 (D) Enraged adj.　　to sieve (全都能抓住)逮捕.理解.對~擔憂
　　→ v.enrage 激怒.使憤怒 →Do you apprehend any difficulty? 是否怕有困難

***Questions 35 through 37*** *refer to the following conversation.*

聽著.有間新餐廳開在對街,我想去試試

M : Hi, Kim.  Listen, a new restaurant just opened across the street.  I was thinking about trying
　　it.  Would you like to have lunch with me?, 你想和我一起午餐嗎? swamp n.沼澤.困境

W : Thanks for the offer, Howard.  I'd love to have lunch with you but I'm <u>swamped</u> here.
謝謝你的提議　　我想跟你吃飯但是這裡太忙了　v.使動彈不得,忙不過來

I'm swamped with work.  Hundreds of letters swamped the company. 好多信寄到
52ⓝ Their company is in a financial swamp. 陷入財政困難.　　　　　公司.

M : Oh, you're handling the Swanson account, aren't you? Well, how about if I grab something for you while I'm out? 你正在處理Swanson的客戶對吧。嗯，還是我出去的時候帶些東西給你吃？

W : Thanks, that's sweet, but I brought my lunch from home today. 真貼心，但我今天有從家裡帶午餐來。 *grab /ɡræb/

35. ( B ) Who are the speakers?
情人 (A) Lovers. *rival 紅
同事 (B) Co-workers.
兄弟姊妹 (C) Siblings. ✓ = compete = vie
對手 (D) Rivals.

v. 抓取、奪取、趕。
Dad grabbed some breakfast and went off to work. 匆匆吃點早餐就去上班了。
→ They vied with each other for the job.
(adj) 競爭的 The rival companies tried to outsell one another. 相互競爭的公司試圖比對方賣出更多的貨物。
(n.) 對手 = opponent = competitor = enemy = foe

36. ( A ) What does the man offer?
帶午餐回來 (A) To bring back lunch for the woman.
帶她去晚餐 (B) To take the woman out to dinner.
幫她做工作 (C) To help the woman with her work.
留著她獨自一人 (D) To leave the woman alone.

37. ( D ) Why does the woman decline?
*concern (A) She doesn't like the man.
✓涉及 (B) She isn't hungry.
使擔心 (C) She has too much work to do.
He is concerned (D) She already has something for lunch.

/dɪˈklaɪn/ v. 委婉的拒絕
decline sb's invitation
② 下降、減少、衰退 / 人的記憶只隨年齡增長衰退
As one grows older one's memory declines.
n. 下降、減少
for her safety. 擔心她的安危 / The news concerns your brother. 消息與你兄弟有關。
(n)關心的事 重要的事

**Questions 38 through 40** *refer to the following conversation between three speakers.*

大家，我們都準備好為了明晚的 RL展 /ˌɛksəˈbɪʃən/ 但是我必須說，我對於
Man UK : So, guys, we're all set for the Regina Lawry exhibition tomorrow night. However, I just have to say—I'm concerned about the placement of some paintings. 一些畫作的擺置有些疑慮

Man US : Which paintings are you talking about? 你在說的是哪些畫作 畫廊那一邊的畫都是黑白的
全黑白系列 a series of attacks / measures 一連串的聲浪、一系列的措施

Man UK : The whole black and white series. I feel like it's dominating that side of the gallery.

W : Hmm. You're right. Perhaps we could break up the series and place them around the 也許我們可以把這系列拆開 並把它們陳列在畫廊四處
gallery. Is this how the artist wanted the paintings to be displayed? 這是畫家們想要的陳列方式
如果我沒記錯，是的。我要看一下她一開始的郵件。但我幾乎確定的（放同一邊）嗎

Man US : If I remember correctly, it is. I'd have to check her original e-mail, but I'm almost
positive. ↔ negative / 明白的。我會打給她看她是否能來畫廊一趟預看展，我們可能可以說服她

W : I see. Well, I'll call her and see if she can come down to the gallery some time this evening 她
to preview the exhibition. We might be able to convince her to change her mind. /kənˈvɪns/ 改變
*He convinced me of his innocence. 他讓我相信他是無辜的。I was convinced that he knew the truth. 意

38. ( B ) Where do the speakers most likely work?
雜誌的出版商 (A) At a magazine publisher. publish v. 出版、發行、刊載、發表、頒布 我確信他知道真相
藝廊 (B) At an art gallery. → publishable adj. 適合發表的
(C) At a café. *了 → publishing house 出版社
(D) At a bookstore. → published material 出版物
→ publisher 出版者、出版公司

GO ON TO THE NEXT PAGE.

39. ( C ) What problem is being discussed? 在討論什麼問題？

cater v.   (A) The artist is unhappy. 藝術家不開心
e ξ

(B) The caterers are late. 外燴人員遲到了

藝術繪師/陳 (C) The placement of some artwork.
列

(D) The arrangement of some flowers.
花朵的安排

— I was so snowed under with work today the I didn't even have time for lunch.

— I can't really take this new project, I am swamped with too much of work.

— I will have to skip this trip as I'm slammed with a lot of work.

— as busy as a bee / beaver

— I'm sorry I can't really help you out with your work this week as I already have a lot on my plate.

40. ( C ) What will the woman most likely do next?

revise   (A) Move an exhibit. 展移地方展
again 00

(B) Revise a schedule. 檢查行程表

= correct  (C) Contact an artist. 核訂
= improve

(D) Write an article. 修正

---

**Questions 41 through 43** refer to the following conversation.

你看起來累累的，你怎麼了？
M: You look tired. What's going on with you?

你不曉得的
W: You have no idea. I'm running around like a chicken with its head cut off. (超忙，停不下來的意思) My kids are at

我一直像被斬頭的雞一樣到處跑

that age now where every day is a marathon of activities. School, soccer practice, violin

lessons, camping trips, baseball games—it never ends! 我的孩子們到了參加鬆式很多活動

的年紀了。學校、足球練習、小提琴課、露營活動、棒球比賽，永遠不曾結束！

M: I hear you. Thankfully, mine are grown up and out of the house. I kind of miss it, you know,

all the excitement. 感謝。我的孩子都已經長大離家了。我還有些掂念呢，你知道的，那些令人興奮的

W: Sure, you can say that now. But remember what it was like to get three hours of sleep a 事

night? 當然，你現在可以這樣說。但記得當時一晚又能睡三小時的日子嗎？

→ = I got you = I'm with you. 我懂你

① 暗指、暗示、意味著

41. ( A ) What does "running around like a chicken with its head cut off" imply?

inhumane  (A) The woman is extremely busy. 超級忙碌  ② 仍然記得

adj. 不人道的  (B) The man is inhumane and cruel. adj. 殘酷的  Rights imply duties.

殘忍的  (C) The woman is terribly shy. /'kruəl/ = mean  權利必然包含義務

(D) The man is nosy and rude. → 超級雞婆  = heartless

好打聽的  無禮的  = brutal

42. ( C ) What are the speakers mainly discussing? → = impolite

(A) Their jobs. 工作  當話者主要在討論什麼？ = rough

(B) Their spouses. 配偶 = mate  = uncivil

(C) Their children. 孩子 = better half  = ill-behaved

(D) Their relationship. 關係 *spoil ①. 寵壞 = to be spoiled by sb.

v. ② 敗壞 : to spoil the view

43. ( D ) What does the woman imply?

(A) Being a parent is no fun. 散步不好玩 ③嬌憤 to spoil sb. with presents

(B) Her kids are lazy and spoiled. 她的孩子很懶並被寵壞 ④毀掉

(C) The man should mind his own business. ↙  to spoil one's chances

(D) She's not getting enough sleep. 他應該管好自己就好了

她沒有得到足夠的睡眠

4

①使火暴炸
你有看到那則巨大蛇爆炸的消息嗎?　explode ②搖晃:The rumor has been
W : Did you see the story about the giant snake that exploded?　戳穿　exploded. 謠言被戳穿了

M : No, I didn't get a chance to check the news. What happened?
沒有,我沒有時間看新聞,怎麼了? 很明顯的,在佛羅里達州有隻巨蟒試圖吃下吃6呎長的鱷魚,牠

W : Apparently, a giant python in Florida tried to eat a six-foot alligator. And he got most of the
把alligator into his belly—but it was too big. Then it just split wide open! 大部分的鱷魚,但真的太大

M : No way! That's incredible. Do they have pictures of it?　然後蛇就爆開了 split-split-split
不可能!太驚人了吧!有照片可以看嗎?　　　　　　　　　　　　　火暴裂,分裂

44. ( B )　What are the speakers discussing?　　　*apparently　=distinctly
　　　(A) Friendly gossip. 隨意的八卦　　　　= obviously　= noticeably
　　　(B) An interesting story. 有趣的故事　　= clearly
財經理論 (C) Financial theory.　　　(消息)　= evidently　= strikingly
自然災害 (D) A natural disaster.　左下　　　= plainly　= manifestly
　　　　　　　　　n.災難,不幸　　　　　　　　　　　= conspicuously

45. ( C )　Why did the snake explode?　　*incredible 難以置信的,驚人的
當局用大砲 (A) Authorities shot it from a cannon.　= unbelievable　= ridiculous
射砲　　(B) It swallowed a bomb.　shoot-shot-shot　= doubtful　= unconvincing
蛇吞下一顆 (C) The alligator was too big.　鱷魚太長了 = questionable　= absurd
炸彈　　(D) Too much gas. 氣太多了

46. ( A )　What does the man imply?　他不相信女生的故事　*terrify v.使害怕,使恐怖
snake　(A) He doesn't believe the woman's story.　→ The girl was terrified
/snek/　(B) He is terrified of snakes. 他超怕蛇　out of her wits. 女孩嚇得
蛇,奸險的人(C) The story is not interesting. 故事一點都不有趣　　魂不附體
snack　(D) He might buy an alligator.　　　→ The thunderstorm
也 小吃,點心 他有可能買一隻鱷魚　　Terrified the child.

這些書是要幹嘛呀? 你在準備考試而唸書嗎?
M : Wow, Lisa! What's with all the books? Are you studying for an exam?
喔,我在唸但不是為了考試. Robert先生要求我寫個關於投資策略的報告
W : Well, I'm studying but not for an exam. Mr. Roberts asked me to write a report about
investment strategies, particularly something called psychometrics. 尤其是心理測量學的.
我知道這件事. 我主修心理學,在轉財經之前. 心理測量學就是用性格測試和評估來做
M : Oh, I know all about it. I majored in psychology before switching to finance. Psychometrics
is all about using personality tests and evaluations to make financial decisions.財經決定

W : Mr. Roberts really should have had you write the report then. I can't make head or tail of
this stuff.他真的應該叫你來寫報告才對. 我根本搞不清楚這些東西的頭和尾巴(不懂)

M : Tell you what. If you want, I could look over your first draft and give you some feedback.
那這樣好了. 如果你願意, 我可以看你的第一分草稿並給你些回饋.

*personality　個性　　　　　　　　　*strategy　strategic
= character　(特徵,特色) characteristic　= planning　adj.戰略上的
= individuality　/kærəktə'rɪstɪk/　= tactics
　　　　　　adj.獨有的

GO ON TO THE NEXT PAGE.

47. ( B ) Who are the speakers?
    (A) Lovers.
    (B) Co-workers.
    (C) Siblings.
    (D) Rivals.

*draft
n. 草稿、通風 Turn the eletric fan on and make a draft.
一口飲盡 He drank the glass of wine at one draft.
吃水深度 The boat has a shallow draft. 這條船吃水淺
v. 起草、設計、徵兵
→ His brother was drafted into military service. 他哥哥應徵入伍.

48. ( D ) What is the woman doing?
    (A) Watching a news report. 看新聞報導
    (B) Studying for an exam. 為了考試唸書
    (C) Reading in her leisure time. 休閒時間看書
    (D) Writing a report. 寫報告

*chastise
≈ 21
= punish = restrain = discipline
I ﹥ I
v. 訓練、訓導 n. 紀律、教養

49. ( D ) What does the man offer?
    (A) To write the report. 寫報告
    (B) To explain psychometrics. 解釋心理測量學
    (C) To chastise Mr. Roberts. 懲罰 Robert 先生
    (D) To read the woman's first draft of the report. 看這女生的第一份報告
    ≈(上)

Questions 50 through 52 refer to the following conversation.

responsible for

W: Hey Bob, it's Alice. Who's in charge of purchasing these days? It's Marge, right? Can I speak with her? 最近是誰在負責採購的? 是 Marge 對吧! 我可以和她聊聊嗎?

M: That's correct. Marge is in charge of purchasing, but she's off this week. I believe her assistant, Greg, is handling it while she's gone. But... he's out to lunch right now. If you need something urgently, as in this moment, go to Pauline in accounting. She can sign off on it.
沒錯, 她在負責採購, 但她這週不在
我想當她不在時是她的助理 Greg 幫她處理. 但是. 他出去用午餐了. 如果你很需要什麼, 在這個時刻, 去找會計部 Pauline 他可以幫你簽.

W: That's OK. No need to go through all that! Do you happen to have Greg's extension?

M: It's 882. 謝拉拉. 但不需要通過那些 (不需那麼麻煩) 你是否剛好有 Greg's 分機?

50. ( C ) Who does the woman ask to speak with?
    (A) Pauline.
    (B) Greg.
    (C) Marge.
    (D) Bob.

*urgently      urgent
adv. 緊急地    adj 緊急的 = pressing = crucial
急迫地         急迫的 = important = vital
                        = exigent = driving
                        / ˈɛksədʒənt /

51. ( C ) Who is Greg?
    (A) Pauline's assistant.
    (B) Alice's assistant.
    (C) Marge's assistant.
    (D) Bob's assistant.

*accounting
n. 會計、會計學
accountant
n. 會計師
account
← n. 帳單、帳戶、客戶

記述 The policeman gave an account of the traffic accident.
解釋說明
John gave us a detailed account of his plan.

根據
理由 He got angry on this account.

56

52. ( A ) What does the woman imply? *hint = infer = suggest*

be tired of   (A) She's not in a hurry to solve her problem. 她不急著解決問題
be sick of    (B) She's tired of people going on vacation. 她很厭煩人們去休假
be sick and (C) She's afraid of Pauline. 她很怕 Pauline
tired of    (D) She's under a lot of pressure. 她壓力很大   *hint v. What are you*
→ Tonny is sick of studying English.     *n. hinting at?*

**Questions 53 through 55** refer to the following conversation between three speakers.

歡迎來到大美國影印店，有什麼我可以幫到你的？

M : Welcome to The Great American Print Shop. How can I help you? 我想要印一些

Woman UK : Hi, I'd like to have some flyers printed for a music festival. 音樂慶典的傳單

沒問題. 資料夾裡有我們設計的模板你可以選擇 → 模板, 模型

M : No problem. This binder contains our design templates for you to choose from.

Woman UK : Actually, I have a hard copy of the design we'd like to use. It's on this USB flash drive. 其實, 我有個電腦列印下來的設計稿我們想用. 在 USB 隨身碟裡面

噢, 店裡的政策是客戶專用我們設計的模板之一, 因為我們的軟體是為那些模板設置的

M : Oh, a shop policy is that customers use one of our design templates because our software is set up for those templates, but let me ask the manager. Suzanne, this customer has her own design. Is that allowed? 但讓我問問經理. 蘇珊. 客戶有自己的設計稿. 是可以的嗎？

Woman US : It is, but it'll cost a bit more because the design will have to be manually entered.
(allowed) 但會多花一點錢. 因為設計是手動輸入的

Woman UK : OK, I don't mind paying extra, but can I get an estimate of how much extra that will cost? 可以的. 我不介意多花錢. 但我可以拿個估價單, 知道要多花多少嗎？

53. ( D ) What are the speakers mainly discussing? *manual adj. 手的. 體力的*
線上付款  (A) An online payment. *refund*       hand
店家退款  (B) A store refund.   n. 退款. 退還    manual labor 體力勞動
電腦更新  (C) A computer upgrade. to get a refund   n. 手冊, 簡介
影印訂單  (D) A printing order.     v. refund    I took the sweater back and
提到了什麼商店政策？     the shop refunded the money.

54. ( C ) What store policy is mentioned?
customer  (A) Services must be paid for in cash. 服務項目要以現金支付
= client   (B) Deliveries must be scheduled in advance. 貨運要事先安排. ③ suspend
= patron  (C) Customers must use a shop design. 客戶要用店裡的設計 使中止, 使停職
= consumer (D) Customers must have a shop account.     The trade with
客戶要有店裡的帳戶 → 經理向客人解釋了些什麼？ that country was

55. ( A ) What does the manager explain to the customer? suspended for ten years.
warranty  (A) An extra charge will be added. 會加上多的收費   He was suspended
保固     (B) An account has been suspended 有個帳戶被暫停使用了 from school for
under    (C) A warranty cannot be extended. 有張保固無法使用了 bad conduct.
under hang  (D) Replacement parts have not arrived. → 因壞行為被
warranty  更換的零件還沒來 ② 使飄浮 有陣煙雲飄在空中 休學
*suspend             燈吊在天花板上 A cloud of smoke was suspended in
v. 懸掛 The lamp was suspended from the ceiling. the air.

GO ON TO THE NEXT PAGE.

**Questions 56 through 58** *refer to the following conversation.*

W : Haven't we met? You're Kahlil Amad from Krunk and Wagg, aren't you? I'm Paige Turner, counsel for Smith, Smith and Joans.

M : Oh, right, of course I remember you, Paige. We met at the Bar Association fundraiser in Peoria. You work with Terry Bull, my roommate from law school. How is Terry, by the way?

W : You have a great memory, Kahlil. Terry's doing great, actually. He's up for partner this year.

M : The guy is one of the most talented litigators in the business. You guys are lucky to have him.

56. ( C ) Who are the speakers?
(A) Teachers.
(B) Volunteers.
(C) Lawyers.
(D) Journalists.

57. ( A ) How does the man know Terry Bull?
(A) They were roommates in law school.
(B) They are from the same town.
(C) They work for the same company.
(D) They both dated Paige Turner.

58. ( A ) What does the woman say about Terry Bull?
(A) He's in line for a promotion.
(B) He's a talented judge.
(C) He's in Peoria.
(D) He's got an unfortunate name.

**Questions 59 through 61** *refer to the following conversation.*

M : Thank you for calling the Apex customer care hotline. How may I help you today?

W : My purse was recently stolen. I need to cancel my Apex Visa card and have a new one sent to me.

M : I'm sorry to hear about that. Give me just one moment. OK, what is the name on the account?

W : Jame Smith. S-M-I-T-H.

59. ( B ) What problem does the woman have?
(A) She lost a close relative.
(B) Her credit card was stolen.
(C) The credit card was declined in a restaurant.
(D) Thieves ransacked her apartment.

58

60. ( D ) What does the woman want to do?
- (A) Get a credit extension. 授信（銀行放款的過程）
- (B) Report a suspicious character. 回報有一各可疑的人物
- (C) Buy a new purse. 買個新錢包
- (D) Cancel a stolen credit card. 取消一張被偷的信用卡

*purse /pɜ˞s/
n. 錢包 手提包 金錢、財源 This piece of china is beyond my purse. 超出我的錢包（買不起）

n. 獎金、捐款
The purse for the next race is $50,000.
v. 皺起
Her lips pursed a little.

61. ( B ) What does the woman imply?
- (A) She misplaced the credit card. 信用卡放錯地方了
- (B) The credit card was in the stolen purse. 卡放在被偷的錢包裡
- (C) Her spending limit is too low. 消費額度 太低
- (D) Everything is always her fault. 每件事總是她的錯

Personal Identification Number

**Questions 62 through 64** refer to the following conversation.

M : Thank you for calling Universal Bank. How may I direct your call? 謝謝你致電環球銀行。我該如何轉接你的電話呢？

W : Um, yes, like, um, I don't remember my PIN number for my debit card. 我忘記我信用卡的密碼了

M : OK, ma'am. I'll transfer your call to a customer service agent. Do you happen to have the card with you? 我會幫你轉接到客服人員你的卡有剛好在身邊嗎？

W : I think so. Wait. This is Universal Bank? Oh, I thought I was calling United Bank. My mistake. 我想是的。啊等等。這裡是環球銀行。我以為我打給美國銀行。我的錯。

62. ( B ) What is the woman's problem?
- (A) She lost her debit card. 信用卡丟了
- (B) She forgot her PIN number. 密碼忘了
- (C) She is lost. 迷路了
- (D) She can't access her accounts. /ˈæksɛs/ 無法登入帳號

Only a few people have access to the full facts of the case. 只有少數幾個人能看到有關該個案全部事實的材料。
接近、進入、使用 門路 進入、使用、存取
*possession /pəˈzɛʃən/

63. ( D ) What does the man ask?
- (A) If the woman has an account with Universal Bank.
- (B) If the woman knows her PIN number.
- (C) If the woman can wait while he transfers the call.
- (D) If the woman has the debit card in her possession.

n. 擁有: The possession of a degree doesn't guarantee you a job. 以責備的狀語回答了
② 自制: With the usual possession, he answered the questions.
in possession 擁有
→ Who is in possession of this? 誰擁有這個？

64. ( B ) Who does the woman need to speak with?
- (A) A sales representative. 銷售代表員
- (B) Someone at United Bank. 美國銀行員
- (C) The man's superior. 他的上司
- (D) A Universal Bank customer service agent. 客服人員

③ 著魔: This charm will protect a man from possession by evil spirits. 護身符保護人不會著魔
人員、代理人、仲介、原動力（被惡魔擁有）
→ I made my assistant my agent while I was abroad. 我出國時請我助理當代理人
agency 部門
Electricity is an important agent in the life of today. 電是生活中一項重要的動力。

GO ON TO THE NEXT PAGE.

你假期有大計劃嗎?
M : Do you have big plans for the holiday? 沒有耶,今年想簡單點,沒有通常的慶祝活動
N : No, not really. We're going to keep it simple this year. None of the usual festivities.
我懂你意思.時機不好.我跟我老婆今年甚至沒有交換禮物
M : I hear you. Times are tight. My wife and I aren't even exchanging gifts this year.
N : Neither are we. Of course, we are still going to have Christmas for the kids, but otherwise,
    we're playing it low key. 我們也沒有.當然.仍有要幫孩子們過節,但除此之外.低調過

65. ( B ) What are the speakers discussing? ✗ otherwise① 不同樣地 We'll get there somehow.
送禮的想法(A) Gift-giving ideas. ①除此以外    by boat or otherwise.
假日計畫 (B) Holiday plans. ② 否則.不然   I'm not feeling well today, otherwise I would
經濟的狀態(C) The state of the economy.    官的.國事的.正式的 do it myself.
他們(D) Their kids. n. 狀態.情勢 v.陳述.聲明 adj. A state dinner was given
他們家今年不會有大肆的假日慶祝活動    in honor of the visiting president.
66. ( A ) What does the woman imply? adj. 奢侈的.浪費的 過度的 Don't be so extravagant;
         (A) Her family will not have an extravagant holiday celebration this year.
假日的慶祝籠(B) Her holiday plans are complicated.    spent your money more
孩子被寵壞(C) Her kids are spoiled and rude.    He hase some extravagant expectations. carefully.
且沒有禮貌(D) Her husband is a cheapskate who doesn't believe in Santa Claus. 他有過度的期待
      吝嗇鬼.    他不相信聖誕老人    (抱有希望)
67. ( C ) What does the man imply? ✗ get along ~    extravagant behaviors
         (A) He and his wife aren't getting along. ①. 離開某地    放肆的行為
他想減肥(B) He is trying to lose weight. ① 過活: We can get along without your help.
沒有很多錢買(C) He doesn't have a lot of money to spend on gifts ③ 進度: How is he getting along
禮物(D) He never really liked the Christmas season.    with his studies.
      他沒有真的喜歡聖誕季節 ④ 和睦相處 He gets along well with his boss.

關於電視台的新員工我有一個問題
Man UK : Hi, Charlotte. I have a question about new hires here at the television station.
N : Sure, Ethan. What's your question?
我覺得我之前有個同事很適合我們的團隊.她在找一個內容產出的職位.我們
Man UK : Well, I think a former colleague of mine would be a good fit for our team. She's 部門有開缺
    looking for a new content producer position and we've got an opening in our department.
    How can I recommend her for the job? 我要如何推薦她來呢?    腳口脖內容/網站內容.
N : Good question. Ah... let's see. Oliver has been here a long time. 聲音.影象.視聽各方面
我剛有聽到我的名字嗎?    Oliver 在這裡很久了呀!
Man US : Yes, did I just hear my name? 你知道如何推薦人給人資部嗎?
N : Yes. Do you know how to refer job candidates to the HR department?
      n. 應試者.應徵者.候選人
Man US : Sure, go to the company website. Find the human resources link, select referrals and
    download the form. Fill it out and submit it to Carol in HR. She'll take it from there.
去公司網站,找到人資部連結.選"推薦"並下載表格.填好後交給人資部的Carol
之後的她會接手

68. ( D ) What does Ethan want to do?
(A) Attend a live broadcast. 參加現場廣播
(B) Request a transfer. 要求轉職
(C) Change a work shift. 換班
(D) Refer a friend for employment. 介紹朋友工作

transfer v. 轉換.校職.搬遷 換車.轉車

*ordinary adj. 善通的.平凡的
n. 尋常.善通.平凡
He is a man of intelligence far above the ordinary.
智力非同尋常的人

69. ( A ) Why does the woman say, "Oliver has been here a long time."?
(A) To indicate that Oliver could answer a question.
(B) To suggest that Oliver be promoted.
(C) To explain a project Oliver is working on.
(D) To express surprise about a mistake Oliver made.

女說 "Oliver已經在這裡很久了" 為何?

指出.表示
指出.說
解釋
表達

adj. 低劣的.不精緻的
His poems are quite ordinary.
他的詩作並不怎樣.

70. ( C ) What does Oliver recommend doing?
(A) Consulting an organization chart. 請教組織圖
(B) Speaking to a manager. 和經理聊
(C) Visiting a website. 去網站看
(D) Picking up an employee handbook. 領員工手冊

Oliver建議做什麼?
consult v. 請教.商議 查閱.看病

(A)說O可以回答問題
(B)說O會升官
(C)解釋O正在做的案子
(D)表達對O所犯的錯的驚評.

→ He consulted his notebook repeatedly during his speech.
→ He went to town to consult his doctor. 他進城去看醫生

handbook 手冊.指南
= manual = guide = booklet
= guide-book = pocket manual

**PART 4**

_Questions 71 through 73 refer to the following introduction._

我們的下一位來賓是第3次上我們節目,並說自己是"一般家庭主婦做了件屬喜的事情
Our next guest is making her third appearance on the program and describes herself
as an "ordinary housewife" who did something extraordinary. She is the author of a
她是本童書作者,賣本成為
children's book that became an international bestseller and is now a popular movie.
僅四年前, P.J. Adams是個待在家裡引個孩子的媽, 當她開始寫
Just four years ago, P.J. Adams was a stay-at-home mother of three when she began
"神秘的魔法" 她說 為了打發時間 她養育的時間是利用
writing _The Wizards of Weird_, in her words, "to kill time." Writing the book while
等小孩從開幼兒園 晚上化們睡著後
waiting to pick up her kids from day care, at night after they were asleep, and in spare
籃球比賽的空檔時間 她從來沒有想過會成為專業書者
moments at basketball games and school plays. Adams never dreamed she'd be
現在她要來宣傳續集了 寺忙的重要
writing books professionally. Now she's here to promote the sequel, _The Importance
下個月推出 但她堅持 成功並沒有改變她
of Being Weird_, due out next month, but she insists that success hasn't changed her.
我們將要持續關注 她仍是個投入的媽媽和妻子
We'll see about that. She's still a devoted mother and wife. Ladies and gentleman,
please welcome P.J. Adams. adj. 專心致志的.忠實的

→ He was still devoted to the study of chemistry. 他仍專心研究化學
→ He is a very devoted husband. 他是位忠實的丈夫
devote v. 將~專廣獻給 He devoted himself to writing. 他專心致志於寫作.

GO ON TO THE NEXT PAGE.

**61**

71. ( B ) Who is being introduced? *extraordinary

在介紹誰? /ɪksˈtrɔːrdnˌɛrɪ/

演員 (A) An actor.
作者 (B) An author. adj. 異常的, 特別的, 離奇的, 特派的
政治人物 (C) A politician. → He strength of will was extraordinary.
電影導演 (D) A movie director. 她的意志力非凡

她很有可能會聊什麼? → He is full of extraordinary ideas.
滿腦子都是奇怪想法

72. ( B ) What will P.J. Adams most likely talk about?

*furnace
工

她的教育 (A) Her education. =special normal
她的新書 (B) Her new book. =unusual ←→ =common n. 火爐, 暖爐
她的宗教 (C) Her religion. =remarkable =standard → infernal
她的孩子 (D) Her children. =exceptional =ordinary adj. 地獄般的

在這次介紹之前, 她曾經在這個節目出現過幾次?

73. ( C ) How many times has P.J. Adams appeared on the program prior to this 大火的

介紹, 識別 introduction? introduce v. → (n.) 備用品 This tire is damaged.

見 (A) Never *spare (adj.) 多餘的, 備用的, 剩下的 Do you have a spare?
引進 (B) One. a spare tire / He is spare of speech. 少說話
引言, 序曲 (C) Two. He has nothing to do in his laboratory
入門書 (D) A dozen. spare time. 空閒時無事可做 (成套的) 設備 photographic +
/ˌæpəˈreɪtəs/
heating apparatus 加熱設備 apparatus

Questions 74 through 76 are based on the following advertisement.

你是否對過分的冬天暖氣帳單覺得煩? → turn the heating off 你不會寧願把錢花在
Are you tired of outrageous winter heating bills? Wouldn't you rather spend that money
其他東西上呢? 那樣的話請記住兩個字 =Pella Windows. 雙層玻璃窗框 (活動窗)
on something else? Then remember two words: Pella Windows. Pella's double-pane
把暖氣留在家裡面, 你的火爐不用一直燒, 你可以省錢 (暖爐)
glass traps heat inside your home, so your furnace works less and you save money.
有Pella保證到省下元, 我們是非常有信心的 可以寫下來, 下次你帳單省來時
We're so confident in our windows that Pella guarantees, in writing, that you will save
會省下至少50%的電費, 不然我們替你付差額 沒到50%
at least 50 percent on your next heating bill or we'll pay the difference. That's right: 50
不然Pella替你付. 保證 只是這樣 若你今天打電話 我們會給你
percent, or Pella pays. Guaranteed. Not only that, but if you call today, we'll give you
比平常便宜25%的安裝費 當你買4扇或者更多窗戶
25 percent off our normal installation price when you buy four or more windows. Our
我們的專業工作人員安裝的又快又容易 你還在等什麼呢?
professional crews make installation quick and easy. So what are you waiting for?
這個冬天不要被巨額暖氣卡住了
Don't be stuck with huge heating bills this winter. Call Pella Windows today at 777-2354
for a free in-home estimate. That's 777-2354. Pella Windows.
免費上門估價 *trap (n.) 陷阱, 圈套, 陰謀, 困境, 活板門

74. ( D ) What is being advertised? → To break out of the poverty trap they need
help from the government.
鋪地毯 (A) Carpeting.
傢俱 (B) Furniture. 為了擺脫貧困的處境, 他們需要政府的幫助
家電 (C) Home appliances. (v.) 落入圈套, 阻止, 落入陷阱
窗戶 (D) Windows.
The bear was trapped. The police trapped him into a confession.
Sand and leaves trapped the water in the stream. 堵住小河的水流

2

75. ( D )   What does Pella guarantee?

(A) Complete customer satisfaction.
(B) Savings of 50 percent on heating bills.
(C) Shatter-proof glass.
(D) Same day installation.

76. ( B )   How much can the consumer save on installation?

(A) 20 percent.
(B) 25 percent.
(C) 40 percent.
(D) 50 percent.

**Questions 77 through 79** refer to the following message.

Hello, Ms. White. This is Joe Lewis from Lewis Construction returning your phone call. You had a couple of questions about the estimate we gave you to remodel your office. First, yes, the quote for the conference room does include installing new carpet and windows. Sorry if that wasn't clear on the estimate. You had also asked why we quoted a range for the cost of lighting. That's because it depends on the type and style of lights you decide you want. The low figure is for standard lighting, and the high one is for the track lighting. As for painting, we subcontract that, so I'll have to check with my painters and see when they can come give you an estimate—hopefully by the end of the week. I'll get back in touch with you about that later today. If you have more questions, give me a call or shoot me an e-mail. My cell phone number is 312-666-0999, and the office is 312-666-0998. E-mail is joe at lewis dot com. Thanks, Ms. White, and have a good day.

77. ( D )   What is the main purpose of the message?

(A) To make a bid.
(B) To file an estimate.
(C) To apologize for a mistake.
(D) To answer questions.

78. ( C )   What is not included in the estimate?

(A) Carpeting in the conference room.
(B) A range of different types of lighting.
(C) Painting costs.
(D) New windows in the conference room.

GO ON TO THE NEXT PAGE.

79. ( B ) What does the speaker say Ms. White can do?

開張支票 (A) Write a check. * negotiate v. 談判·協商·洽談
回電給他 (B) Call him back. /nɪ'goʃɪ,et/ The government will not negotiate
和畫家協商 (C) Negotiate with the painters. with the terrorists. 不願恐怖分子談判
給估價 (D) Give an estimate. [D] 順利通過 Negotiate a deep river.
成功渡過一條深河.

**Questions 80 through 82** refer to the following recording.

這是個公平的問題(該問的問題), 而且不用油腔滑調的辯駁, 答案是肯定的, 你們當中
有些人在今年年底以前會沒有工作.
That's a fair question, and not to be glib but the answer is yes, some of you are going
但是我們有計劃 現在在這個困難的
to be out of a job before the end of the year. But we have a plan. Now, in this tough
經濟狀況下, 我們和客戶的行為一樣, 拉緊腰帶並找尋方法來省錢
economy, we're going to act just like our customers—tightening our belt and looking
我們將尋找方法來節省能源, 更有效的運作我們的店
for ways to save money. We'll be looking at ways we can conserve energy, operate
並且整合新的流程來減少勞力成本
our stores more efficiently, and integrate new procedures that cut labor costs. We're
我們也要重新檢視我們的定價結構 我們也許可能要降價並且
also going to re-examine our pricing structure. We might have to lower prices and
有一陣子靠更少一點的利潤 我們重視每一位員工
operate on a thinner profit margin for a while. Now, we value each and every one of
我們不會讓你們任何一個人走, 直到我們先試了所有可能的 辦
our employees, and we won't let any one of you go until we've first tried everything we 法
possibly can. So I can't say who among you will be laid off, but rest assured that we're

be devoted to     by all means
committed to avoiding it at all costs. 所以, 我無法說你們當中誰會被解雇
dedicated to     at any price  但是保證 我們會致力於不計任何代價來避免
這樣的情形發生 (解雇大家)

80. ( A ) Who is the speaker?
公司執行長 (A) A corporate executive.
銷售人員 (B) A sales clerk. 開除 Steven was cashiered in 1985.
出納員 (C) A cashier. ①出納員 ⓥ撤~的職 他在1985年被免職
(D) A parking lot attendant
停車場管理人員 → attendant ⓝ隨員·侍者. a queen's
care 人 服務人員 attendant

81. ( D ) What is the speaker talking about?
順手牽羊 (A) Shoplifting. ⓐⓓ 護理的·出席的·伴隨而來的
廣告 (B) Advertising. One of the difficulties attendant on shift
健康照顧 (C) Health care. work is lack of sleep. 輪班工作制帶來的困難
存錢 (D) Saving money. 之一就是睡眠不足.

82. ( D ) Which of the following is NOT part of the speaker's plan?
縮減勞力 (A) Cutting labor costs. * conserve We turned the bicycle lights off
成本 (B) Conserving energy. v. 節省·保存 to conserve the batteries.
省能源 (C) Reducing profit margins. → He is trying to reduce expense.
(D) Hiring new employees.
=減少利潤 顧用新員工 The cancer victim was reduced to skin and
癌症患者瘦得皮包骨 bones.

reduce v. 減少 = lessen = decrease = cut ↔ increase
變弱 = lower = diminish = moderate

4

As you know, we've got a deal with ABC Technology School to provide discount computer classes for our staff. Even though these classes are free to our employees, some of you have complained that workers in your department aren't taking advantage of them. Staff have complained that they are too tired and too busy to drive to the ABC campus after work. But I have a hunch that most of them don't recognize the benefit expanded computer skills will have for their job performance. I can understand this, since most of them already have the skill they need to perform their current jobs well. So, we've decided to be proactive and bring the classes to the employees. Starting immediately, ABC will send an instructor to our offices for twice-weekly classes.

83. ( A ) Who is the speaker most likely talking to?

(A) Department managers.
(B) New employees.
(C) Stockholders.
(D) Computer instructors.

84. ( B ) Why are some staff members not taking advantage of the classes?

(A) They can't afford them.
(B) They are not convenient.
(C) They start too early.
(D) They don't like the instructors.

85. ( A ) What did the speaker do to solve the problem?

(A) He arranged for on-site classes.
(B) He cancelled the classes.
(C) He gave bonuses.
(D) He made attendance mandatory.

This is Ursula Ogden with a 3 p.m. KPIX traffic update. At the moment there is a huge backup on southbound Interstate 5 near the MacArthur Avenue exit, due to a car-truck collision. Police and emergency crews are on the scene, and it looks like it's going to take awhile to clear it up. The right two lanes are blocked, but the two left lanes are open, and there's a police officer directing vehicles. Northbound traffic on 5 is also

*GO ON TO THE NEXT PAGE.*

bottle-necking through that area as drivers slow to take a look. But that congestion should ease in a few minutes, as we see traffic authorities getting ready to switch the special express lanes from southbound to northbound at 3:30. Traffic on other major roadways looks normal at this hour. This is Ursula Ogden and you're listening to KPIX. Traffic is brought to you by Tasty Oatmeal, the breakfast that provides a full day's supply of 14 vitamins and iron. It's not just oatmeal, it's tasty! Stay tuned for news and weather after this word from our sponsor!

86. ( D ) When was this report made?
 (A) At dawn.
 (B) Mid-morning.
 (C) Noon.
 (D) Mid-afternoon.

87. ( A ) What is causing the back-up in the northbound lanes of Interstate 5?
 (A) People slowing down to look at the accident in the southbound lanes.
 (B) Police and emergency crews.
 (C) Tasty Oatmeal.
 (D) An overturned truck carrying thousands of empty bottles.

88. ( B ) What will listeners hear next?
 (A) An advertisement.
 (B) The weather report.
 (C) The traffic report.
 (D) A musical performance.

Questions 89 through 91 are based on the following announcement.

Thank you all for coming. After considering several factors, including the survey you completed last quarter, we've decided to implement four-day workweeks, beginning next month. We will operate 10 hours a day, from 8 a.m. to 7 p.m., of course with an hour for lunch, on Monday through Thursday. The office will be closed Fridays and throughout the weekend. Though we will still work 40 hours a week, we estimate that this change will reduce our energy use by 30 percent, and will also save each of you, on average, about $50 a month in gas and transportation costs. Overall, this change will significantly reduce our company's carbon footprint. To save even more energy, we will be installing energy-efficient fluorescent light bulbs throughout the building, starting next week.

During the changeover period, we understand that some of you, particularly those with young children, might need special accommodations as you adjust to a four-day week. We'll be happy to help you any way we can.

在這個轉換期間，我們明白你們有些人，尤其是那些有小孩的可能需要特別的安置，因為要調整、適應一週四天的上班方式，我們很樂意提供你需要的任何協助。

講話的人宣佈什麼？

89. ( A )  What is the speaker announcing?

上班時間有變 (A)  A change of working hours.
有耗更能能源 (B)  A plan to consume more energy. → 給有小孩員工的日照設置  accommodate
(C)  A daycare program for employees with young kids.  v. 容納、通融、給方便
要發出去的 (D)  A new questionnaire to be passed out.  住在校內/外 → The hotel can accommoda
新問卷  to fill out the questionnaire  * campus  500 tourists.

90. ( C )  What will happen on Fridays?  n. 園區、校園  to live on campus
政府單位來 (A)  A government official will visit the campus.  adj. 校園的 Do you like campus life?
拜訪 (B)  The light /bʌlb/ bulbs will be changed.
換燈泡 (C)  The office will be closed. 辦公室會關  * promising
(D)  Employees will go home at 6:00 p.m. 員工6:00回家  adj. 有希望的、有前途的、大有可
現在每週員工工作幾小時？  a promising sign 好的跡象的
a promising artist
91. ( D )  How many hours will employees now work per week?  * lead n. 指導、榜樣、線索、訊
(A)  10.   * In fact = as a matter of fact
(B)  15.   ⎰ = in effect    = as it is  → Who is playing the lead in t
(C)  20.   ⎱ = in reality  = to speak the truth  play?
(D)  40.   = in truth  → All the children followed his lead.

**Questions 92 through 94** refer to the following advertisement.

你對於目前的工作還滿喜歡？ 也許該是時候做些改變了呢？ 我們可以幫助你
Are you happy with your current job?  Maybe it's time for a change?  We can help.  I'm
我是職業媒合總裁  比刻是好的時間讓我們幫助
Sammy Govic, president of Career Match dot com, and now is a great time to let us
你找尋到你夢想中的職業  夢想到、想到、夢見  我們的專業工會
help you search for the career you've always dreamed of.  Our professional staff will
協助你、一步步更新履歷  張貼到網路上，回覆廣告
assist you step by step in updating your resume, posting it online, answering ads, and
然後代替你的身力、搜尋成上萬的工作列表  不浪費你的時間
searching through thousands of job listings on your behalf.  Instead of wasting your
看數以百計的廣告  讓我們展現給你看如何只專注於
time reading hundreds of advertisements, let us show you how to focus your search
取得到最好的機會 (未來最有可能發展的工作)  會持續告訴你最新的雇用趨勢
on only the most promising leads.  We'll keep you updated on the latest employment
並教你如何寫能夠抓住眼球 (吸引人) 的履歷  能增加你在面試中得分的
trends, and teach you how to write an eye-catching resume that will increase your
up. 事實上我們甚至會訓練你面試技巧  機會
chances of scoring an interview.  In fact, we'll even train you in interview techniques.
我們過去10年已教育了 (幫我工作) 已經數以千計的人找到工作，你還在等什麼？
We've placed thousands of people over the past 10 years.  What are you waiting for?
打給我們  我足到 careermatch.com 找我們
Call us now at 1-800-929-9292, or visit us online at Career Match dot com.

* dream up 憑空想像、編造        * dream sth. away 虛度光陰 / 把虛度一生
→ Trust you to dream up a crazy     → She dream her life away,    一事無成
scheme like this! 虧你想得出這種    never really achieving anything.
異想天開的計畫。

GO ON TO THE NEXT PAGE. ➡

92. ( B ) What is being advertised?
商品 (A) A product.
服務 (B) A service.
學校 (C) A school.
職缺 (D) A job opening.

*effect    n. 效果, 效力
out | make, do
/ɪˈfɛkt/
effective    adj. 較好的, 生效的
/əˈfɛktɪv/

93. ( D ) What is suggested about Career Match dot com?
當地的公司 (A) It is local.
可負擔的 (B) It is affordable.
老舊的 (C) It is old.
有效的, 起作用的 (D) It is effective.    out | make

infect    v. 感染
Into |
infection    n. 感染, 傳染
infectious    adj. 有傳染性的
adj.

94. ( C ) What does the speaker suggest listeners do?
給2週時間 (A) Give their two-week notice.
寄出履歷 (B) Send in their resumes.
致電或去官網 (C) Call or visit the website.
準時出現 (D) Show up on time.

proficient    adj. 熟練的
forward |
proficiency    n. 熟練, 精通

Questions 95 through 97 refer to the following tour information and brochure.

大家可以注意一下公車前面嗎?    希望大家每個人都很享受
OK, folks. Can I have your attention at the front of the bus? I hope everybody enjoyed
我們歷史上著名的 Greenbriar 區的建築導覽    我們看到一些很棒的東西
our architectural tour of the historic Greenbriar District. We saw some amazing stuff,
對吧!    現在如果你往右邊看    你會看到 Shipley 小餐館    就是我們享用午餐
didn't we? Now if you look to the right, you'll see the Shipley's Inn, where we'll have
的地方    1835年建立    一開始是郡法院    根據我們的行程表
lunch. Constructed in 1835, it was originally the county courthouse. And according to
我們準時到達    當你下巴士的時候, 我會發小手冊
our schedule, we're right on time. As you get off the bus, I'll pass out brochures with
裡頭有資訊關於你在 Sears Building 會看到什麼, 這棟樓是全市最大報商的起源
information about what you'll be seeing in the Sears Building, home of the city's largest
同時, 讓我提醒你, 不要留私人物品在巴士上當我們下車時
newspaper. Also, let me remind you, do not leave any personal items on the bus when
並且要經過旅程中都要留心那些個人用品
we disembark, and keep track of those personal belongings throughout the tour.
away | embark v. 上船, 從事, 著手 They embarked on a campaign to get people to vote.

95. ( C ) What does the speaker say about Shipley's Inn?    展開一場動員人們投票的活動
有異國結果 (A) It serves exotic food.    /ɪgˈzɑtɪk/ adj. 外來的, 奇異的
有多個地點 (B) It has multiple locations in the area.    *architectural adj. 建築學的
以前是法院 (C) It used to be a courthouse.    architecture    n. 建築學, 建築術
最近有得獎 (D) It has recently won an award.    architect    n. 建築師.

*courteous    法院
→ courtesy    adj.
n. 禮貌    有禮貌的, 體諒的

covet 貪求 → covetous adj. 貪婪的
/ˈkʌvɪtəs/

96. ( B ) Look at the graphic. What time is this talk most likely being given?
- (A) At 10:00 A.M.
- (B) At 12:00 P.M.
- (C) At 1:15 P.M.
- (D) At 4:00 P.M.

```
TOUR SCHEDULE
------------------------
Greenbriar District  10:00 A.M.
Lunch  12:00 P.M.
Sears Building  1:15 P.M.
Exploration Museum  4:00 P.M.
========================
```

97. ( C ) What does the speaker say she will distribute?
- (A) Bottles of water.
- (B) Maps.
- (C) Brochures.
- (D) Umbrellas.

*Questions 98 through 100* refer to the following excerpt from a meeting and garden layout.

Thanks for attending this planning meeting for the new community garden. I'm Edward, and I'm the coordinator of this project. Here's the layout for the new garden. We'll mostly be planting perennial flowers and ornamental shrubs, but we will have a vegetable garden, too, and we're going to plant that first. The vegetables are going to go in the plot immediately to the left as you enter the garden. Also, I need volunteers to help me on Saturday. I'd like to put up a fence around the perimeter of the garden. The wood for the fence will be delivered that morning.

98. ( B ) Who is the speaker?
- (A) A security guard.
- (B) A project coordinator.
- (C) A course instructor.
- (D) A news journalist.

GO ON TO THE NEXT PAGE.

99. ( D ) Look at the graphic. Where will vegetables be planted?
    (A) Plot 1.  *plot n.小塊土地        → plot out 分配.規劃.描繪
    (B) Plot 2.        陰謀.情節        You should plot out your time
    (C) Plot 3.                        properly. 應合理分配自己的時間。
    (D) Plot 4.   v.策劃.密謀
                      → The rebels plotted against the government.
                                  策意要推翻政府。

反叛者 Plot 2

Toolshed

Picnic area          Plot 1

Plot 4

Plot 3

Entrance

100. ( B ) What does the speaker plan to do on Saturday?
    (A) Take some photographs.        He has been installed
    (B) Install a fence.  v.安裝.設置.使就職 → in his new office. 他已就任新職
    (C) Lead a tour.        It is necessary that you install a burglar alarm.
    (D) Attend a picnic.        你有必要裝防盜警報器
  參加野餐
                      → installation
*attend                ┌ n. 裝置.就職.軍事駐地
  to 傾
  v.陪同.伴隨.護送        * installment payment 分期付款
      護送.出席.照料
I'll attend to the matter. ┘→ The installation of a new mayor.
  我來處理此事              新市長的就職
You're going out?        a heating installation 暖器設備
But who will attend to the baby?
  誰來照料這個Baby?

**NO TEST MATERIAL ON THIS PAGE**

*GO ON TO THE NEXT PAGE.*

In the Reading test, you will read a variety of texts and answer several different types of reading comprehension questions. The entire Reading test will last 75 minutes. There are three parts, and directions are given for each part. You are encouraged to answer as many questions as possible within the time allowed.

You must mark your answers on the separate answer sheet. Do not write your answers in your test book.

**PART 5**

**Directions**: A word or phrase is missing in each of the sentences below. Four answer choices are given below each sentence. Select the best answer to complete the sentence. Then mark the letter (A), (B), (C), or (D) on your answer sheet.

*Handwritten annotations (top):* 106. 強而有力的暴風雨吹倒了2根電線桿並連根拔起了好幾棵大樹 (B) furnish v. 佚應了家具. 給房間配置傢俱 How are you going to furnish the house? (C) upbraid = scold = reproach 辱罵了(抓起罵了) = condemn Her boss upbraided her for being late. 因遲到罵他 107 (C) He took all the money and left me high and dry. 他拿走所有的錢, 讓我個 We searched high and low for the lost watch. 找到處找手錶 用境 There is no need to be so high and mighty with me! 用著對我擺架子 我們的泰國之行意外的價格划算.

101. If you really want something in life, you have to work ------- .
(A) from it
(B) of it
(C) for it
(D) off it

*Handwritten:* C / 如果生命中有某樣你真的很想要的東西. 你必須努力爭取! go for it. just do it. make it happen

105. Our trip to Thailand was ------- inexpensive.
(A) quietly
(B) surprisingly
(C) radically
(D) gently

*Handwritten:* B / a good but inexpensive wine (reasonable) 好. 而且不貴=廉價的 quite 相當 ≠ cheap ≠ radical adj. 根本的. 徹底的 These developments have effected a radical change in social life. 徹底地 這些發展使社交生活發生根本的改變. 根本地

102. The box is ------- heavy for my grandmother to carry.
(A) many
(B) much too
(C) a lot
(D) little

*Handwritten:* B / 這箱子對我奶奶而言太重了搬不動 You're too nice to help the kid. It's too dangerous to drive fast on busy streets. 但並非此用法 (祝詞用法) 有的了程也有too, to 虛主詞 受主詞

106. The powerful storm downed two power lines and ------- several large trees.
(A) uprooted
(B) unfurnished
(C) upbraided
(D) undated

*Handwritten:* A / (上) 連根拔起的 沒有擺家俱的 責罵的 未填日期的

103. His inability to learn another language was a(n) ------- to his success.
(A) obstacle
(B) pothole
(C) detour
(D) shortcut

*Handwritten:* A / 他沒有能力學習另一種語言對他的成功而言是項阻礙是A = barrier = barricade 洞 = impediment = hindrance 岔道 = interdiction = forbiddance 走逕 決定 A

107. Hank's interest in Monica seems to ------- at random.
(A) come and go
(B) came and went
(C) high and dry
(D) back and forth

*Handwritten:* 漢對Moni的興趣好像來來去去 The pain in my leg comes and goes. 我的腿有時疼有時不疼. 處於困境(上) 來來回回

104. Night after night, he came home ------- an empty house.
(A) on
(B) at
(C) in
(D) to

*Handwritten:* D / 夜復一夜. 他回到空無一人的屋子 (C) She was very supportive when I lost my husband. 我失去丈夫時她給我很多支持. I don't think it a supportable idea. During this difficult time, his friendship made life supportable to me.

108. We should willingly take risks in ------- of new projects.
(A) supporting
(B) support
(C) supportive
(D) supportable

*Handwritten:* A / 我們應該負願(樂意)承擔風險在做新案子時 v. n. ← (C) supportive adj 支援的. 贊助的 ← (D) supportable adj. 可支持的. 可贊成的

*GO ON TO THE NEXT PAGE.*

109. The defunct NASA satellite is expected
to fall back to earth ------- days. 人造衛星
C
(A) with 失去作用的NASA衛星預計幾天內
(B) without 會掉回地球
(C) within *The judge suspected the witness was*
(D) withhold *withholding information.* 法官懷疑證人有
保留阻擋 *He's holding his approval.* 他不肯同意.所保留.

110. Consider all the possibilities -------
C making a decision. 在做決定之前考量到所有情
(A) until *think twice*
(B) instead *look before you leap* 況
(C) prior to ↔ posterior to
(D) as *I'll walk with you*
*as far as the post office.*
→ defunct adj. 死的.非現存的.已廢止的

111. Management is thinking of ------- our
main office to Taipei. 管理階層在思考把新辦公室
D 指派 (A) appointing *to* 搬到台北
勝過 (B) outplaying *necessary adj. 必要的.必需的*
部署 (C) deploying *in esa, seri n. 必要的物品.必需品*
搬家 (D) relocating

112. The risks and side effects of using
D painkillers ------- nausea, headaches, and
fever. *respire 呼吸 反胃*
邀請 (A) invite *conspire 同謀*
想要 (B) intend +to → *He intends his son to manage*
鼓勵 (C) inspire +v-ing → *I intend study the company*
包含 (D) include +for *abroad.*
→ *The trap is intended for you.*
使用此痛藥的副作用包含了反胃.頭痛和發燒

113. ------- it was a holiday, Eric went to the
office to finish an important project.
A (A) Even though 雖然是假日, Eric去辦公室
(B) Instead *adv.* 完成一個重要的案子. *protest*
(C) So *n. protest*
(D) During *抗議.反對*
這部電影積極入圍過很多獎項.包含最佳原創劇本奧斯卡金像獎

114. The film has been nominated for many
honors (hand)
-------, including the Academy Award for
Best Original Screenplay. 腳本=script
要求 (A) demands → 紀念物.紀念碑.紀念館
尊重 (B) respects *adj. 紀念的 a memorial speech*
獎項 (C) honors → *n. 榮譽. 面子.禮儀.光榮的人/事*
(D) memorials
*使增光: You honor us with your presence.*
v.
14 尊敬 *He honors his teachers.* 兌現: *He honored his promise.*

115. More jobs means ------- people looking
for work. 更多的工作需求意味更少的人在找工作
C (因為大家都有工作了)
(A) farther
(B) further → 距離 > adj.
(C) fewer → 程度 adv.
(D) faster
*Do you need further help?*
*We'll help you further.*

116. You can play computer games ------- your
homework is finished. 只要你的作業寫完了
B (A) as far as 就可以玩電腦遊戲
(B) as long as 只要 *You can borrow the book*
(C) as well as 也 *as long as you keep it clean.*
(D) as good as 這件事等於是解決了
幾乎等於. 不遜於. 實際上 *The matter is as good as settled.*

117. The national spelling bee was won by a
------- girl from Texas. 全國的拼字比賽是由
B (A) fourteen-years-old 位14歲女孩贏得
(B) fourteen-year-old 那便你沒有整理星擋案
(C) fourteen-year-old 如果你把它們都存放在
(D) fourteen-old 一個地方,當需要時你可以
-year

118. Even if you don't organize your files, if 整理
you keep all the records in one place, 出來
B you can sort them out when necessary.
(A) where ①整理 *This room needs sorting out.*
(B) when ②解決問題 *I'll leave you to sort this*
(C) while *problem out.*
(D) which ③收拾某人 *I'll soon sort him out.*
為你而設的圈套 *Just let me get my hands on him.* 等我到他款

119. Beijing has announced that it will open 收拾他
two new parts of the Great Wall of China
to meet high tourist demand
(A) protest 北京宣佈會開放高里長城的2
(B) outrage 個新部分來符合高度旅遊需求
(C) demand 暴行 n. *They committed*
(D) order 秩序.順序 *outrages on innocent*
v. *citizens.*

120. Tim ------- fourteen, sometimes sixteen,
hours a day. Tim一天工作14.有時16小時
B (A) work *Such conduct outrages*
(B) works *our rules of morality.*
(C) have worked 那樣的行為違反了
(D) is work 我們的道德規則.

21. Our ~~flight~~ leaves at eight o'clock, so we better head for the airport around five.
(A) journey 我們的飛機8點離開，我們最好
(B) sight 五點鐘去不幾場。
(C) travel Out of sight, out of mind! 眼不見為淨
(D) flight shortsighted, nearsighted, myopia, farsighted, hyperopia 廣泛的

*[handwritten left margin: D 航程 眼光 旅行 班機]*

22. Though racial ------- was common in the past, it is no longer tolerated in our society. 雖然種族歧視在以前很普遍
(A) palpitation 可是在我們社會中已不被容許
(B) sterilization Sterile adj. 貧脊的 不肥沃的
(C) discrimination judge 兩個住在市中心最
(D) localization 鐘的問題就是噪音和 (消過毒的) = barren 在地化 汗染。除此之外 非常方便的。

*[handwritten left margin: C 心悸 發科]*

123. The two main ------- of living downtown are the noise and pollution. Otherwise, it's very convenient.
(A) pullbacks 徹退 = pullout = withdrawal
(B) fallbacks = disadvantage = flaw
(C) drawbacks 缺點 = shortcoming
(D) outbacks 人口稀少開發落後的邊疆地區

*[handwritten left margin: C 拉回 障礙 阻撓]*

沒有證據指出馬雅人相信世界會在 2012/12月結束
124. There is no evidence to suggest the Mayans believed the world would ~~end~~ in December 2012. * bend 彎曲。屈服。致力
(A) bend → The boys bend their attention on
(B) friend making model ships. 致力於做船模型
(C) end → She tried to bend her husband
(D) send to her wishes. 她設法使丈夫順從她的 願望

*[handwritten left margin: C]*

你知道我要寄這個包裹去法國需要多少郵資嗎？
125. Do you know how much ~~postage~~ would need to mail this package to France?
(A) postage → (n) 重量，負擔，重要性
(B) weight → That's quite a weight off my mind. 如釋重負
(C) tape
(D) flight → Our boss's opinion seem to carry very little weight at home. 老闆的意見在家裡似乎沒有什麼權威
→ She was weighted down with cares. 她心事重重.

*[handwritten left margin: A 郵資 (V) 加重重於 壓迫]*

126. Practical applications of alchemy produced a ------- of contributions to medicine and the physical sciences.
(A) wide range 錬金術的實際軍用
(B) broad stripe 提供大量的貢獻對於
(C) vast divide 醫療和自然科學
(D) long road 嚴重分歧/物理的 身體的 自然的

*[handwritten: A 廣泛的 寬條紋 akemI]*

127. Many critics have tried to ------- the economic recession on the President's domestic policies. 很多評論家都試圖
(A) blame 把經濟衰退怪到總統的
(B) list 國內政策 depression
(C) correspond → downturn
(D) fault lay put the blame on place

*[handwritten: A]*

128. Scott had all ------- of problems in school.
(A) sights Scott在學校裡有各種問題
(B) sorts = kinds * correspond
(C) sizes Your actions should correspond
(D) styles with your words. 表裡如一

*[handwritten: B]*

早在CEO的辭職正式宣佈以前就知道了.
129. The employees ------- about the CEO's resignation before the announcement was made public. resignation
(A) know n. 辭職 /rɛzɪg'neʃən/
(B) knew 放棄 → They accepted the
(C) knowing 屈從 situation in resignation.
(D) have known 無可奈何的接受了現狀

*[handwritten: B]*

遠不是 He is far from smart = He is stupid.
130. Far from being a shrinking violet, Lucy has many strong ------- which she is not afraid to express. 絕對不是個害羞的人
(A) opinions Lucy 有很多頑硬的 (堅持的)
(B) decisions 想法. 她不怕表達
(C) clues
(D) theories Shrinking → shrink 縮小，畏怯 violet /vaɪəlɪt/ 紫羅蘭

*[handwritten: A]*
→ She shrinks from meeting strangers. 他怕見生人

shortage of hands has shrunk our plant's yearly output. 人手不足使我們廠年產量減少

GO ON TO THE NEXT PAGE.

# PART 6

**Directions**: Read the texts that follow. A word, phrase, or sentence is missing in parts of each text. Four answer choices are given below each of the texts. Select the best answer to complete the text. Then mark the letter (A), (B), (C), or (D) on your answer sheet.

Questions 131-134 refer to the following notice.

*這台 3D 印表機是平面設計部門員工專屬的. 其他部門的工作人員必須使用標準印表機.*
*放在二樓. 平面設計部門員工每週*
*在無需主管授權的情況之下可以*
*列印至多 5 個物件.*

**AGX Industries**

**3-D Printer Policy**

*(一般的)*

*exclusive*
This 3-D printer is for the ------- use of Graphic Design Department
131.

employees only. Workers from other departments must use the

standard printers found on the second floor. Graphic Design

Department staff members may print up to 5 objects per week

without a manager's authorization. Staff must receive managerial

*additional*
approval to make ------- items. *若員工需要多印, 要有管理階層的同意*
132.

*請注意, 3D印表機只能* 132.

*Is Intended ──→用於研發和業務使用*
Note that 3-D printing ------- for development and business purposes
133.

*個人的列印是不允許的*
only. No personal printing is permitted. -------
134.

*③[D] 有點不舒服的 = I'm feeling a bit peculiar.*
Thank you for your cooperation.
*他用一天種奇特眼神看著我.*

*① He looked at me with a very peculiar expression.*
*adj. 奇怪的. 親的 ② I have my own peculiar way of doing things.*

**131.** (A) peculiar *我有自己獨特的做事方式*
(B) unusual
(C) customary *It's customary to tip the waiter.*
(D) exclusive

*adj. 添加的. 額外的*
**132.** (A) additional
(B) required *require v. 需要*
(C) such *The roof requires repairing.*
(D) these *This project will require less money.*

*(C)用 3D 印表機印出來的東西*
*是給 Convex 實驗室和外部行銷同仁內部使用*
*(D)技術支援部門維護所有的列印機和印表機.*

**133.** (A) is intended
(B) should intend
(C) intends
(D) intending

*(B)二樓的販賣機 9月時會被更換*
*replace v. 取代. 代替. 歸還*
*I'll replace the cup I broke. 我會賠*

*(A) LED 螢幕已升級為視網膜螢幕 (更清楚)*

**134.** (A) The LED monitors have been upgraded to
retina screens *二樓自動販賣機 9月會換新*
(B) The second-floor vending machine will be
replaced during the month of September
(C) Objects created with the 3-D printer are for
internal use by Convex Labs and external
marketing associates *用3D印表機印的物件*
(D) Technical Support maintains all printers
and copiers *只使內部和外部行銷影件使用*
*技術支援 維護所有的印表機和複印機*

我們建議要預約
因為在Richmond的飯店
住宿非常有限.

www.hotelcartier.com/richmond/reservations

# Hotel Cartier Richmond
## Reservations

We recommend reservations because hotel accommodations in Richmond are very limited.
**135.**

保留預訂要付一晚押金或者全部房費的一半(若住超過一晚表)
Reservations will be held with a one-night deposit or 50 percent of total room charges for stays of longer than one night. Cancellations made more than seven days prior to your scheduled arrival date -- will be refunded -- in full.
**136.**
預訂入住日期7天以前取消. 將會退還全額

若.車於某些原因. 您預計入住日期七天之內需要取消, 你整個住宿期的費用將被收取.
If, for some reason, a reservation must be cancelled within one week of your scheduled arrival date, charges for the entire -- length -- of your stay will be billed to you. --------.
**137.**          **138.**

*limit
n.界線. 無法容忍的人.事 That man is the limit. 那人真叫人無法容忍.
限度: He knows his own limits. 能知道能力到哪兒

(V) 限制. 限定
→ n. limitation = obstruction
= restriction = barrier
= restraint = inhibition
= impediment = damper
= obstacle

135. (A) limits   He has pushed my patience
  (B) limited   to the limits.
  (C) limitation   他已讓我忍無可忍
  (D) limiting

137. (A) area
  (B) height
  (C) length
  (D) sense

136. (A) are refunding
  (B) had been refunding
  (C) will be refunded
  (D) were refunded

提早離開也是一樣(沒有提早說都要收錢)
138. (A) This policy applies to early departure as well
  (B) In addition, we will soon open another hotel in Richmond
  (C) We hope that you have enjoyed your stay
  (D) Hotel guests may also purchase these items through room service.

*GO ON TO THE NEXT PAGE.*

17

New Message _ / x

To    EveryWear Customer Support

Subject:   Order EW-098911

To Whom It May Concern:

I recently purchased an all-weather rain jacket from the EveryWear clothing website. When I first received the jacket a month and a half ago, I tried it on and put it in my closet. -------, when I went to wear it in the rain for the first
**139.**
time yesterday, I noticed slight defects in the stitching of the hood, causing it to seep moisture. I know that any ------- items must be returned or exchanged
**140.**
within three days and that my purchase is no longer within the required time frame. ------- If it ------- out since I checked, I would be happy to choose
**141.**        **142.**
another jacket at the same price.

Please let me know what my options are.

Sincerely,
Maggie O'Connor

Sans Serif / B / U / 臺 畺 畺 / ll

Send

---

**139.** (A) Still
(B) However
(C) Therefore
(D) Additionally

**140.** (A) accepted
(B) ill-fitting
(C) mistaken
(D) defective

**141.** (A) This policy has been extended to at least 60 days
(B) Nevertheless, I am asking you to kindly make an exception
(C) Please add a credit to my account to be used for future purchases
(D) I sent the package back to you two weeks after I received it

**142.** (A) be selling
(B) having been sold
(C) has sold
(D) will sell

18

Kimberton 集團週二時宣佈將以 2 億 34 萬的金額買下 Helios Energy 公司.

Kimberton 發言人說公司預計明年底之前 將利潤翻番兩翻

## Kimberton to buy Helios Energy manufacturing division

merger : A+B=B / Consolidation A+B=C
acquisition : A 併 B 看起來仍是兩間但其實一間

財務專家相信這購 HE 會使 Kimberton 成為
世界領頭的橡膠製造商

HOUSTON—Kimberton Group LP announced Tuesday that __它__ would purchase Helios
**143.**
Energy Corp. in a deal valued at $230 million.

*analyst /'æn!ɪst/ n. 分析者
'analysis n. 分析. 解析
百萬

A spokesperson for Kimberton said the company expects to double its profits by the end of next year. It will accomplish this by making full use of Helios Energy's recently updated manufacturing facilities. __(B)__
**144.**

要完成這個目標, 將會
使用 Helios Energy 最近更新的
生產設備

*maintain v. 維持、主張: He maintains that he once saw a ghost.
保養. 侍養: He maintains his son at college.

Financial experts believe the Helios Energy acquisition will make Kimberton the world's leading producer of industrial rubber. "They will be well ahead of their __-----__," said top analyst J.
**145.**
Walker White. 頂尖分析師 J. Walker White 說他們會領先對手們.

工業的
勞資的
產業的 adj.
competitors
對手

Kimberton plans to maintain Helios Energy's current workforce, with each of Helios Energy's factories continuing normal operations for the next five years. __-------__, Kimberton will
**146.**
evaluate whether additional staff are needed.

計畫要保留
目前的人力
讓每間 HE 的工廠持續維持
正常運作
在接下來
After that time
5年之內

在那之後, Kimberton 會評估
是否需要多的員工.

(B) 所有四間都是最大功能運作. (有幾機開幾機)

(C) 另一間公司明年將會被併購.

**143.** (A) it    *reject ⓥ 拒絕. 去除. 丟棄. 否決. 駁回
A (B) he    The patient's body rejected the heart
(C) those    病人的身體排斥移植的心臟 transplant.
A) (D) someone    'reject n. The rejects were
其他公司給的職缺都被拒絕了.    stacked in a corner.

**144.** (A) Offers from other firms were rejected
B (B) All four are operating at maximum capacity 廢物
(C) Another company will be acquired next year 堆在角落
(D) The transaction should improve morale

**145.** (A) critics 評論者
C (B) suppliers 供應商
(C) competitors 競爭者
(D) investors 投資者

如你所要求

**146.** (A) As you requested
D (B) As a matter of fact 實上
(C) After all 畢竟
(D) After that time 在那之後

這筆交易應該會增進士氣.    v. 改進. 增進. 提高. 利用機會
she improved her leisure by learning foreign languages. 利用閒暇時間 國外語

# PART 7

**Directions**: In this part you will read a selection of texts, such as magazine and newspaper articles, e-mails, and instant messages. Each text or set of texts is followed by several questions. Select the best answer for each question and mark the letter (A), (B), (C), or (D) on your answer sheet.

**Questions 147-148** refer to the following invitation.

*[handwritten notes:]*
throw
give } a party
hold
dress code 衣著規定
business } casual 需領帶
semi } formal 不需領帶

## Shh, it's a surprise...

### Dennis Flynn

*Dennis要50歲了，但不想要別人知道*

is turning 50 and he doesn't want anyone

to know about it.

*但不管怎樣我們要幫他辦一個 party.*

147 But we're throwing him a surprise party anyway.

*× be surprised at  對~感到吃驚 意外    ×surprise*
*I was surprised at his winning the race.    (n) 驚；詫 To my surprise,*

Friday, July 17 at 7:30 p.m.
*he refused to cooperate*

Ruth's Chris Steakhouse, 23 Broad Street, New Orleans *with us.*

148 Dress code: business casual  *令我吃驚的是，*

*× surprise*                                 *他不肯和我們合作。*
*(V) 使吃驚感到意外*        Please, NO GIFTS!

*I was surprised to learn that he was taking drugs. 聽說他在吸毒，我很*

RSVP before July 16 to Vera Flynn via e-mail only! *吃驚.*

Flynn.vera@gmail.com

*× purpose*
*n. 目的 What is the purpose of his visit? 他來訪的目的是什麼?*

*v. 決意，打算: He purposes to visit Taipei. 他打算訪問台北*

*邀請函的目的為何?*

*服裝規定是什麼?*

**147.** What is the purpose of the invitation?  *邀請函的目的*

(D) (A) A wedding. 婚禮
(B) A concert. 演唱會
(C) A charity dinner. 慈善晚宴
(D) A surprise party. 驚喜派對

**148.** What is the dress code?

(C) (A) No gifts. 不用禮物
(B) July 16. 7月16
(C) Business casual. 休閒商務
(D) Via e-mail only. 只透過 e-mail

20

G: General

PG : Parental Guidance suggested
護

PG 13: Parents Strongly Cautioned
輔

R: Restricted 限制級

\* feature

(n) 特色, 特徵

This is the key feature of our product.

面貌, 相貌
特別報導, 專欄

The local newspaper ran a feature on child labor.

地方報紙登載一篇有關童工的文章.

(v.) 以~為特色
由~主演 → The new movie features two of my favorite actors.
以~為號召

## THE SUPERSTAR CINEPLEX
### Wilshire and Normandy        Los Angeles

### NOW SHOWING!

**THE BLOB** (PG) n. 一滴, 一團
starring Rosie O'Donnell
Weekdays only: 12:00, 3:30, 7:00

cruise 巡航        bruise 瘀青
**CRUISIN' FOR A BRUISIN'** (NC-17) 17歲以下不得入場
starring Adam Lambert and Clay Aiken
12:30, 3:00, 5:30, 8:00

鋸子        主演
**SAW 73 (R)** starring Brooklyn Beckham as "The Saw"
Weekdays: 8:00, 10:00   Sat-Sun 7:30, 9:30, 11:30

促銷方案
DATE NIGHT PROMO DEAL
ADMIT ONE  Buy two (2) tickets before 6:00 p.m. for any feature
and receive a free small popcorn
晚上6點以前買任何一部電影2張票送一盒免費小火爆米花

ex 誰有資格得到小的爆米花?

149. Which of the following is NOT a show
D    time for "The Blob"?
     ＊電影院
     (A) Monday 12:00.
     (B) Wednesday 3:30.  movie
     (C) Thursday 7:00.   theater (theatre)
     (D) Saturday 7:00.   movie house
                          movie palace
     cinematic            cinema
     adj. 電影的

150. Who is eligible for a free small
B    popcorn? law 任何有買兩張票的人
     (A) Anyone who buys two tickets.
     (B) Anyone who buys two tickets
         before 6:00 p.m. 任何6:00前買兩張
     (C) Anyone who buys a ticket. 票的人.
     (D) Anyone on a date. 任何買票的人
     任何在約會的人        的人.

GO ON TO THE NEXT PAGE.

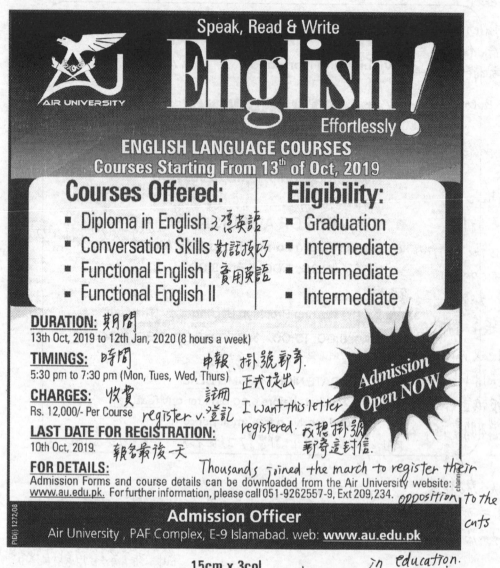

**Speak, Read & Write**

# English!

*Effortlessly*

AIR UNIVERSITY

**ENGLISH LANGUAGE COURSES**
**Courses Starting From 13ᵗʰ of Oct, 2019**

## Courses Offered:
- Diploma in English 文憑英語
- Conversation Skills 對話技巧
- Functional English I 實用英語
- Functional English II

## Eligibility:
- Graduation
- Intermediate
- Intermediate
- Intermediate

**DURATION:** 期間
13th Oct, 2019 to 12th Jan, 2020 (8 hours a week)

**TIMINGS:** 時間
5:30 pm to 7:30 pm (Mon, Tues, Wed, Thurs)

**CHARGES:** 收費
Rs. 12,000/- Per Course
register v. 登記

**LAST DATE FOR REGISTRATION:**
10th Oct, 2019.
報名最後一天

申報、掛號郵寄.
正式提出
註冊
I want this letter registered. 我想掛號郵寄這封信.

**Admission Open NOW**

**FOR DETAILS:**
Thousands joined the march to register their opposition to the cuts

Admission Forms and course details can be downloaded from the Air University website: www.au.edu.pk. For further information, please call 051-9262557-9, Ext 209,234.

**Admission Officer**
Air University , PAF Complex, E-9 Islamabad. web: **www.au.edu.pk**

PID(I) 1272/08

15cm x 3col

in education.
數千人參加遊行表示反對削減教育經費.

如何得到入場表格和課程

在廣告什麼?

**151.** What is being advertised?
C
- (A) A college scholarship. 大學獎學金
- (B) A travel package. 旅行套裝行程
- (C) English language courses. 英語課
- (D) An art school. 藝術學校 英語課

**152.** How can the admission forms and 資訊?
C course details be <u>obtained</u>? 去獲得或給至
- (A) By going to the main office.
- (B) By request via air mail. 用航空郵件請
- (C) By downloading them from the 我 Internet. 從網路上下載
- (D) By October 10th.
  before

X 閒逛. 慢條斯裡的做事: He loved to potter around in the garden.
potter v. 閒
n. 陶工
陶藝家                                                          他喜歡在花園裡做些瑣碎事

# Potter Valley
# Park and Camp Ground

urban adj ↔ rural
                                                          rustic
以下活動需要許可證
**Permits are required for:**          = metropolitan
都市的    **Urban camping** 都市搭帳篷    = municipal    * consumption
     - **Alcohol consumption** → 飲酒    n. 消耗. 用盡. 消費
明火  - **Open flames (including BBQ grills)** This food is for our
以下活動是禁止的    含BBQ烤架 prohibited  consumption on the trip
**The following are PROHIBITED:**                      這些食物供旅途中吃
汽車  - **Motor vehicles (except in parking lot)**
火器. 槍枝 **Firearms (no exceptions)** 無例外    除了在停車場的
放大的聲音 **Amplified sounds** amplify v. 放大. 增強. 擴展
喝酒  - **Alcohol consumption (except by permit)** 除非有許可
玻璃容器 **Glass containers**    ample adj. 大量的. 廣大的
高爾夫. 游泳 **Golfing, swimming, diving** ampliation n. 擴張. 擴充
**Drug possession or trafficking**
擁有毒品或走私 possess v. 擁有. 佔有    traffic v. 走私. 非法買賣
**Pets:**                                    → a drug trafficker 毒品走私販
需要拴住 **Leash required**
之後要清理 **Please clean up after** → The man trafficked with the natives
                                       for ivory 和當地居民買賣以取象牙
請做回收並妥善的丟棄垃圾
# Enjoy our parks!    He has trafficked in drugs
**Please recycle and dispose of trash properly** for many years.
**These rules and regulations are enforceable by law.** 販賣毒品多年
這些條規受
法律限制 Mariposa County Department of Parks and Recreation
enforce v. 強迫    forceful adj. 有力的    reinforce v. 增加
          power
forced adj. 被迫的    forcible adj. 強迫的. 強而有力的
                    I heard a forcible arguement in favor of the

哪一項不需要許可證?
**153.** Which of the following does NOT
D    require a permit?    permit
    (A) Urban camping.    = allow
    (B) Alcohol consumption. = give the green    forbid
    (C) Open flames.    light to ~    = ban
    (D) Pets.
                    = disallow

**154.** Which of the following is NOT new
A    prohibited?    keep    policy.
    (A) BBQ grills. 我聽到對於新政策
    (B) Firearms.    強而有力的論據
    (C) Glass containers.
    (D) Amplified sound.

GO ON TO THE NEXT PAGE.

*reject v. 拒絕 → rejection    eject v. 排斥 → ejection n. 排斥.驅逐.噴出
deject v. 使沮喪 → dejection    inject v. 注射 → injection

Dear Sally,

我已經結婚9年了. 我和我先生都有接受教育並且職業很成功. 我們有個現在15歲
I have been married 9 years. My husband and I are educated and

和前夫的女兒, 以及兩個我們自己的孩子
successful in our careers. We have a daughter, now 15, from my previous

and        我先生很愛我的女兒. 對待她
marriage as well as two children of our own. My husband loves my daughter

像自己的孩子一樣.    可是, 我的姻親 (公婆)
and treats her like his own child. My in-laws, however, have never accepted

my daughter as a grandchild. 從來沒有接受我的女兒為他們的孫女.

他們喜歡我們兩個較小的孩子並且扮演祖父母的角色. 一有機會就會.
They enjoy our two younger children and play grandparents to them

他們很想很快希望小孩在他們那裡過夜, 而且總是打電話
every chance they can. They want to have the little ones sleep over soon and

來問他們是否好        他們從來沒有談到過我的女兒.
they always call to ask about them. They never mention my daughter. They

從來沒有送我女兒卡片或禮物, 但都有送結兩個小的.
never send my daughter cards or gifts but do send them to the two little ones.

我的先生告訴過他們. 拒絕我的女兒如何傷了我的心. 他們很防禦 (反應誇大)
My husband has told them how their rejection of her hurts me. They

但也沒有改變過 (上)    現在, 今年夏天我們要搬
have been defensive about it, and have not changed. Now, we are moving

離他們近一點的地方.    當我們打電話要和他們討論時,
closer to them this summer. When we called to discuss this with them, my

我婆婆開始在電話那頭哭, 泣說她沒有做錯任何事
mother-in-law started crying on the phone saying that she hasn't done

anything wrong. I don't want them in our lives if they can't treat all the

children the same. Help!  我希望他們在我們的生活裡. 若他們無法對所有
孩子一視同仁。    *defensive adj. 保護的. 防禦的

—*Stuck in the Middle*                              defend    v. 保護.防禦 翻繼續

*nosy adj. 好管閒事的 The old lady is very nosy.
/'nozɪ/    愛追問的.    So nobody likes to talk to her. → She defended herself successfully
                                                                        in court.
寄件者主要的問題是什麼?                                為何這個問題變得更緊急?

155. What is the sender's main problem?        157. Why is this problem becoming
C   (A) Her husband is having an affair. 老公有外遇    more urgent? 她又有3別的孩子.
    (B) Her in-laws are very nosy. 她公婆很愛八卦     C (A) Stuck in the Middle is having
    (C) Her in-laws don't accept her daughter.         another child. 她老公所請離婚
    (D) Her in-laws are spoiling her kids. 公婆不接受   (B) Stuck in the Middle's husband
spoil /spɔɪl/ v. 寵壞她小孩          她女兒          filed for divorce. 她家要搬近一點
156. What happened when she tried to discuss          (C) Stuck in the Middle's family is
A   the problem with family members?                  moving closer to the in-laws.
    (A) Her mother-in-law started crying. 婆婆開始哭   (D) Stuck in the Middle's daughter
    (B) Her father-in-law promised a fresh            can't sleep at night.
        start. 公公答應會有個新的開始 / n.發脾氣. 發怒  她女兒晚上無法睡覺。
    (C) Her daughter threw a temper tantrum. 她女兒發脾氣  *urgent adj. 緊急的. 急迫的
    (D) Her husband told her to shut up.              = pressing = vital = essential = imperative
老公叫他閉嘴

An American hitchhiker who claimed to have been a victim of a drive-by shooting while gathering material for a memoir on kindness actually shot himself, likely to draw publicity to his project, police said. Ray Dolin originally reported to police that he was hitchhiking along a rural Montana road when the driver of a pickup truck pulled up next to him and shot him for no apparent reason. A man driving a pickup truck that matched Dolin's description of the alleged shooter's vehicle was subsequently arrested. Dolin later admitted to police that he had shot himself, and the charges against the man arrested for the shooting have been dropped.

158. What was Ray Dolin doing when he claimed to have been shot?

(A) Writing.
(B) Driving a pick-up truck.
(C) Filing a police report.
(D) Hitchhiking.

159. What do we know about Ray Dolin?

(A) He is well-traveled.
(B) He is very kind.
(C) He shot himself.
(D) He enjoys hitchhiking.

160. What happened to the man Ray Dolin falsely accused?

(A) He died of wounds suffered in the gunfight.
(B) He was arrested and later released.
(C) He left the state of Montana and is now considered a fugitive.
(D) He wrote a memoir about kindness.

GO ON TO THE NEXT PAGE.

**Contract for Purchase of a Car**

Buyer's Name                          Seller's Name
Address                               Address
City, State, ZIP                      City, State, ZIP
Phone                                 Phone

The Seller hereby conveys to the Buyer full ownership and title to the motor
vehicle described below:

Description of Motor Vehicle Sold:

Year _____  Make _____  Model _____

VIN: _____

The Buyer hereby agrees to pay the Seller $_____ on (  /  /20), and

$_____ on the _____ th day of each month beginning (  /  /20), until all

payments made to the Seller total $_____

If Buyer fails to make a payment on or before its due date, a late fee of

$_____ shall be added to the balance due and shall be payable immediately.

Both parties hereby agree that this is an "as-is" sale, with no warranties of any
kind expressed or implied.

This agreement shall be governed by the laws of the State of _____ and the

County of _____ and any applicable U.S. laws

The parties hereby signify their agreement to the terms above by their signatures
affixed below:

_____                    _____
Buyer's signature, date               Seller's signature, date

**161.** What is the purpose of this contract?

(A) Property rental.
(B) Security clearance.
(C) Construction estimate.
(D) Purchase of a car.

**162.** Who is the contract between?

(A) The county and the state.
(B) The Department of Motor Vehicles.
(C) Buyer and Seller.
(D) Year, make, and model.

**163.** What do both parties agree to?

(A) This is an "as-is" sale with no
warranties.
(B) To complete all payments within
one year.
(C) Shared ownership of the vehicle.
(D) Laws of the county come before
those of the state.

Questions 164-167 refer to the following article.

Crime dramas are fun, engaging and entertaining to watch, but is it possible that they cause more harm than good? The tremendous popularity of television shows like "Crime Scene Investigators: Miami" (CSI) have gone a long way toward building interest in the field of forensic science and crime scene investigations, but there may be a downside. There is a concern among the forensic science and law enforcement communities that the technology and tactics presented in these shows have led to unrealistic expectations about police capabilities among the public at large and, even worse, potential jurors.

The "CSI effect" is a term applied to the increasingly pervasive idea that criminal cases can be wrapped up in an hour and that there is always incontrovertible proof of guilt available. While it's true that great advances have been made in the area of forensic science, it's unrealistic to expect a crime scene to be processed, evidence analyzed and a conclusive forensics report to be completed before the detective or criminal investigator assigned to the case gets back to the office after leaving the scene.

Unfortunately, though, that is what many victims expect, and what a lot of juries now look for. When they don't see it, defense attorneys often exploit the lack of DNA or other smoking gun evidence in an effort to make it appear as though law enforcement investigators didn't do their job. (Usually, though, nothing could be further from the truth.)

164. What is the main result of the "CSI effect"?
(A) People living in poor areas are afraid of the police.
(B) Modern technology makes solving crimes a slam dunk.
(C) People have developed unrealistic expectations about solving crimes.
(D) Police work seems glamorous and entertaining.

165. What has caused the "CSI effect"?
(A) Urban legend.
(B) Television programming.
(C) Popular opinion.
(D) Scientific research.

166. Where would this article most likely be found?
(A) In a sports magazine.
(B) In a cable television guide.
(C) In a journal of psychology.
(D) In a book of exotic recipes.

167. According to the author, who uses the "CSI effect" to their advantage?
(A) Criminals.
(B) Crime scene investigators.
(C) Forensic scientists.
(D) Defense attorneys.

GO ON TO THE NEXT PAGE.

**Questions 168-171** refer to the following report.

In a bad mood? Don't worry—according to research, it's good for you.

An American psychology expert who has been studying emotions has found being grumpy makes us think more clearly. In contrast to those annoying happy types, miserable people are better at decision-making and less gullible, his experiments showed. While cheerfulness promotes creativity, gloominess breeds attentiveness and careful thinking, Professor Michael Callahan told Colorado Science Magazine. The University of Denver researcher says a grumpy person can cope with more demanding situations than a happy one because of the way the brain "promotes information processing strategies". Professor Callahan asked volunteers to watch different films and dwell on positive or negative events in their life, designed to put them in either a good or bad mood. Next he asked them to take part in a series of tasks, including judging the truth of urban myths and providing eyewitness accounts of events. Those in a bad mood outperformed those who were jolly—they made fewer mistakes and were better communicators. Professor Callahan said: "Whereas a positive mood seems to promote creativity, flexibility, cooperation and reliance on mental shortcuts, negative moods trigger more attentive, careful thinking and paying greater attention to the external world."

168. What is this report mainly about?
(A) Psychology.
(B) Decision making.
(C) Mythology.
(D) Multi-tasking.

169. What does Professor Callahan say about grumpy people?
(A) Their ability to relax is compromised.
(B) Their moods are influenced by others.
(C) They are better communicators than happy people.
(D) They are more creative than happy people.

170. Which of the following is NOT promoted by a positive mood?
(A) Creativity.
(B) Careful thinking.
(C) Cooperation.
(D) Flexibility.

171. Which of the following is promoted by a negative mood?
(A) Attention to detail.
(B) Creating eyewitness accounts.
(C) Gullibility.
(D) Cheerfulness.

28

**Marita Leroy (10:37 A.M.)** 財務長剛剛要求我出席公司的年度預算審察會.
I was just asked by the financial officer to sit in on the firm's annual budget review. Therefore, I can't make our 3:00 P.M. meeting today.
因此, 我3:00時無法去開會。

**Kevin Ambari (10:38 A.M.)** 那我們可以早一點練習明天的客戶展示嗎?
Could we practice tomorrow's client presentation earlier? What about reserving the conference room at 1:00 P.M.? 約1:00的會議室可以嗎?

**Dan Collins (10:39 A.M.)** 對我來說那樣是比較好的. 我4:00要離開去看醫生
That would be better for me anyway. I need to leave at 4:00 PM for a doctor's appointment.

**Marita Leroy (10:39 A.M.)** 沒那麼好運. 我正在看行程表. 今天下午都約滿了
No such luck. I'm looking at the schedule now—it's booked solid all afternoon.

**Kevin Ambari (10:40 A.M.)** 那何不下午兩點時你們都來我辦公室?
Then why don't you both come to my office at 2:00? We can run through the presentation and slideshow here. 我們可以在辦公室跑一次報告和幻燈片.

**Dan Collins (10:41 A.M.)** 聽起來很不錯哦. 我要去 Audio-Visual 部門借
Sounds good. Should I get a projector from the A/V dept.? 投影機嗎?

* see you    catch you later         talk to you later       so long
改天見    在短時間內就會再見面      之後再聊         即將離開或送人出國

**Kevin Ambari (10:42 A.M.)** farewell    祝一路平安, 送親友深造, 旅行    I'm off
Don't bother. We can look at the slides on my computer screen. =I'm leaving.
不用麻煩了, 我們可以用我的電腦螢幕看就好了.    是對方自己要離開

drop it    * Ciao 原本是義大利文
ignore it                後英文也常用

**Marita Leroy (10:43 A.M.)**             見面/道別皆可用
OK. See you later.    it doesn't matter
聽見/見 see you soon.    it's all right
      see you around.

* I gotta hit the road. I gotta head out.    Until we meet again.
我得走啦?                                後會有期, 畫不捨說再見, 日後必再見

GO ON TO THE NEXT PAGE.

**172.** Why is Ms. Leroy <u>unavailable</u> at 3:00 P.M.? 為何她3點沒空

C

(A) She has a phone call with important clients. 她和重要客戶講電話
(B) She has to <u>give a presentation</u>. 她要演講
(C) She has been asked to attend a meeting. 她被要求參加會議
(D) She has a <u>medical</u> appointment. 她有和醫生約

* medical adj.
醫學的. 醫療的 / n. 健檢 I have to have a medical

**173.** At 10:42 A.M., what does Mr. Ambari before going most likely mean when he writes, "Don't bother."? 當她寫下這句話時,什麼意思? abroad.

D

(A) He should not be <u>disturbed</u> this afternoon. 他今年下午不該被打擾
(B) Ms. Leroy should not <u>reserve</u> a room. 他不該預約房間
(C) Mr. Collins does not have to come to a meeting. 他不需要來參加會議
(D) Mr. Collins does not need to bring a projector. 他不需要帶投影機來.

**174.** Why does Mr. Ambari suggest using his office? 為何他建議使用他的辦公室

D

(A) Because it can <u>accommodate</u> a lot of people. 因為可以容納很多人
(B) Because it is located near the <u>finance office</u>. 因為離財金辦公室近
(C) Because his <u>audiovisual</u> equipment has been upgraded. 近
(D) Because the conference room is <u>unavailable</u>. 因為會議室無法使用 abroad.
因為視聽教材已更新

**175.** When will the three people meet?

B

(A) At 1:00 P.M.
(B) At 2:00 P.M.
(C) At 3:00 P.M.
(D) At 4:00 P.M.

③ 通融. 給方便
The policeman
→ accommodated us

* accommodate when we asked for help.
  ə a ə e
①能容納.提供膳宿
②使適應.使相符
→ You will have to accommodate yourself to the changed situation.
你必須適應變化的形勢.

* available ⟷ unavailable
  ə e ə
① adj. 可用的. 在手邊的 = convenient = handy = at hand
→ The swimming pool is available only in summer.            = obtainable
② 可得到的. 可買到的
→ Is there water available around here?
③ 有空的
→ The director is available now.
④ 有效的
→ The voucher is no longer available.

* finance
/ˈfaɪnæns/
n. 資金
→ the finance page 財經版
  the finance minister 財政部長
            ministry 財政部
finance
ɪ æ  n. 財政. 金融. 財務狀況
       v. 融資. 提供資金

* disturb
①妨礙. 打擾    ②使心神不寧 → She was disturbed to hear you had been injured in the accident.
→ I'm sorry to disturb you so early.       她聽到你在事故中受傷感到不安
② 擾亂      他們被指控擾亂公共治安

30 → They were charged with disturbing the public peace.

## Letter 1

Dear Dr. Stein,

I am applying for the Congressional Scholarship, a $10,000 annuity to be awarded to a single student. Given that my enrollment at Harvard is dependent on my receiving financial aid, this would be a wonderful opportunity for me.

The recipient of the scholarship must demonstrate both ability and direction in his or her field of study. In order to assess such qualities, the scholarship committee requires that applicants submit at least one reference letter from a professor in their major department.

Would you do me the honor of submitting the reference letter required for the application?

I took your International Law class in the fall semester of 2017, and your Global Organization class in the spring of 2018. I received an A in both classes.

All scholarship materials must be submitted by November 30, and I enclosed an addressed, stamped envelope for your convenience. The addressee on the letter should be Scholarship Director Ogden Chalmers. I will be stopping by during your office hours this week to confirm. Meanwhile, if you need to speak with me directly, I can be reached at (650) 323-9826.

Appreciatively,

Louis Langer

**Letter 2**

Dear Director Chalmers,

One of my best and brightest students, Louis Langer, is
applying for the Congressional Scholarship. It is my opinion that
Mr. Langer is an excellent candidate for the award in question; he
has proven himself to be well-qualified in every facet of the
scholarship requirements, both in my classes and elsewhere on
campus.

　　Having served as a professor at Harvard for over two decades,
I have had the opportunity to observe some exceptional students.
Louis Langer is one of those rare students who manages to stand
head and shoulders above the rest, in a highly competitive
environment. In my classes with Mr. Langer, namely International
Law and Global Organization, he has exhibited deep insight into the
world of finance and law. He has an excellent attitude and work
ethic, which will no doubt form the foundation of his education.

　　I might add that I am aware of other professors' opinions
regarding Mr. Langer, and to my knowledge, they are in accordance
with mine. That is, Louis Langer is the superior choice to be the
recipient of the Congressional Scholarship.

Sincerely,

Dr. Stu Stein, Professor Emeritus Law
Harvard University

---

*Handwritten annotations:*

apply v.
applicant
application n.

我最棒以及最聰明的學生之一 Louis Langer 要申請

國會獎學金

我的想法是 Langer 是這個

正在討論中的獎項的絕佳候選人　討論中

他已經證明了自己在這個獎學金的要求門檻上各個面都符合

∝ I = aspect 層面

不論是在我的課堂裡還是校園的其他地方.

身為哈佛的教授超過20年的時間

我有機會能夠注意到一些表現卓越的學生

Louis 就是那些能夠站得比別人高看得比別人遠的學生之一

在這樣高度競爭的環境裡他也可以

Langer 在我的課上

也就是國際法和全球組織

他展現出了深度的洞察力對於

世界財金和法律

=showed 他有完美的態度和工作道德

毫無疑問的是由於他教育的良好基礎

我可能增加一些我注意到其他教授對於 Langer 的想法

而且就我所知 他們的想法和我是一樣的

也就是說，Louis 是接受這分獎學金最棒的人選

∝ I I ∝ (adj) 較高的,較好的,不為~

人　receive v. 收到,得到,歡迎,接受　(n) 長官,長輩,佔優勢者　所慾的

① His speech was well-received. 他的演講很受歡迎

施比受更有福.

② It's more blessed to give than to receive.

He is superior to bribery. 他不受賄賂.

* in accordance with

① 依照 ② 與~一致

/braɪbərɪ/ n. 行賄,受賄

他遵照他父親的願望把錢捐給了學校.

In accordance with his father's wish he gave the money to the school.

76. Who is Louis Langer? ✗reference ⓝ提及
B (A) A lawyer. 律師                           涉及
(B) A student. The book is for reference 參照. 出處←
(C) A doctor. ⓥ提到. 指出 only. 本書僅供參考.
(D) A banker. → Success seems to have little
reference to merit. 成功與品質
似乎沒有多少關聯.

77. What did Louis Langer ask Dr. Stein
B to do? 更改成績了
(A) Change his grade.
(B) Supply a reference. 提供參照 (推薦信)
(C) Demonstrate a product. 展示商品
(D) Cancel his subscription. 取消訂閱
under write

78. How do Louis Langer and Dr. Stein
C know each other? 在同間公司上班
(A) They work at the same firm.
(B) They are college roommates. 大學室友
(C) Louis attended Dr. Stein's classes. 上上S的課
(D) Dr. Stein married Louis' sister.
S娶了L的姐/妹

80(D) Louis太有錢了 以至於不能收到財務補助
wealthy = rich                  = abundant
ⓓ有錢的 = affluent   ⓢ豐富的 = ample
      = prosperous   充分的 = replete

177(B) supply v. 供給. 提供
n. 供給, 供應, 庫存, 供應品
→We have new supplies of our coats.
   有新進貨的皮大衣
生活用品. 補給品. 車糧
Our medical supplies are running short.
   醫療用品快用完了
   個人生活費
My father has cut off the supplies.
   父親停止給我生活費了

179. What did Dr. Stein do in response to
A the request? 他如何回應這個請求?
(A) He wrote the reference.
(B) He rejected the idea. 拒絕了
(C) He gave the task to a colleague.
(D) He looked up Louis Langer on
Facebook. 上臉書搜尋Louis
把任務交給同事

180. What is Dr. Stein's opinion of Louis
C Langer? S對L的看法是什麼?
(A) Louis is a lazy student. 他很懶
(B) Louis is a sensitive individual.
(C) Louis is an exceptional student.
(D) Louis is too wealthy to receive
financial aid.
是個脾氣易生氣的人   感光的. 機密的
                       易受影響的. 過敏的
✗sensitive adj. 敏感的. 易怒的
→ The child is sensitive to egg.
   對雞蛋過敏
I need some sensitive paper.
   需要一些感光紙.
He is sensitive about his failure.
   人家一提他的失敗他就生氣
Anna is sensitive to strong smells.
   對強烈氣味很敏感

(C) Louis是很棒的學生
exceptional adj. 例外的. 異常的. 特殊的
out  fake
(特別不一樣的要拿出來)
→ The fireman showed exceptional
   表現非比尋常的勇敢  bravery.
exception n. 例外. 反對. 異議
→ He works every day, with the
exception of Sunday. 他每天工作, 除了
                              週日

GO ON TO THE NEXT PAGE.

33

*modify v. 修改 We have to modify our plan a little bit.
a 改工 緩和 He has modified his demands. 他已降低了他的要求

→ modification n. 修改 = The plan requires some modifications.

→ modified car 緩和 = With the modification of his anger he could think clear again.
n. 改裝車 他的怒氣漸消又能清晰地思考.

**MEMO**

To: Department Heads ②未解決的 ① 傑
From: Deborah Lynn 未完成的,未償付的 決 → = distinguished = noticeable
的 = prominent = significant
Date: December 8, 2018 表現良好員工有多的年假 = eminent = striking
Subject: Annual Bonus Leave for Employees with Outstanding Performance
→ The outstanding debts must be paid by the end of the month.

6月1号開始 我們會推出以下的有薪年假政策修正方案 未了的債務月底前要償還
Starting January 1, we will introduce the following modification in our company
每一年會1個部門有一各員工可因優受表視
policy regarding annual leave (paid vacation). Every year, one employee from
被頒予特別休假.
each department will be awarded a special bonus leave for outstanding
① 有資格的,合法的 He is eligible for retirement. 合乎退休條件.
performance. ②合適的 Helen married an eligible bachelor. 嫁給了個合意的單身漢
得到資格的員工特會有5天的年假從1月5号開始
The eligible employees will have five (5) days of annual leave credited on
out law 多的年假和一般年假是分開算, 直到使用之前都有效
January 15. The bonus leave will be accounted for separately and will remain
儘管其他的年假限制仍會繼續 (休假段規定依然要遵守)
available until used, notwithstanding any other limitation of annual leave that
繼續 發揚 融入 歸然,儘管= Notwithstanding he tried hard, he failed in
may be carried forward. 還是=Notwithstanding the bad weather, the match chemistry
went on.
12/5, 10:00 我們會開會討論2018表視評估的結果並且確定最後的得獎名單
We will have a meeting on December 15 at 10:00 a.m. to discuss the results of
同意,贊許,批准,認可
the 2018 performance evaluation and approve the final list of eligible employees.
→ The professor does not approve the government's
會議之後就會對員工宣布 foreign policy. 教授不贊同政府的外交政策
The announcement will be made to the employees following the meeting. If you
若你有任何問題或考量 就在會議前通知我
have any questions or concerns, please contact me prior to the meeting.

*concern v. 涉及,關係到,影響到,使擔心,使不安
n. 關心的事,重要的事,擔心,掛念,關懷 The news concerns your brother.
There is no concern of mine. 這消息和你弟弟有關
不關我的事 He is concerned for her safety.
Andrew expressed his concern. 他擔心她的安全/又 他對她很關心
表示了他的關切. He was very concerned about her.

34

*scapegoat n. 不是負的替人頂罪, 而是被指派出來去做大家不想做的事, 說大家不想說的
(替死)

To: "Deborah" < el_queso_grande@cxt.com > *individual

From: "Pete Sears" < oh_no@cxt.com > adj. 個人的: The director of the factory felt no
個別的　　　individual responsibility for the
deficit.

Subject: Annual Leave Memo

Date: 12/12/18　就我方立場而言, 這分合約的關鍵導在於它的　廠長個人不覺得
罰款條款　應對工廠虧損負責
→ As far as we are concerned, the sticking point
of this contract is its penalty clauses.

Deborah,

我有機會坐下來和 Ron 跟其他幾位部門頭頭討論這次的休假政策, 而我被選為
(up)　代罪羊 (183)

I had the chance to sit down with Ron Booker and a couple of the other

department heads to discuss the bonus leave policy, and I was chosen as scapegoat

來提出幾項疑慮　不是每個人的立場我都同意
to raise a few concerns with you. I don't agree with everyone on some of these

談判的關鍵點　所以請記得一句老話 "不殺先生" 'ædɪdʒ' = saying
sticking points, so please keep in mind the old adage, "Don't shoot the messenger."

超過一個以上的部門主管認為這是個壞主意
1. More than one department head believes the new policy is a bad idea, at least

至少他們覺得在他們各自的部門裡多是壞主意　(up)
they perceive it to be a bad idea within their individual departments. Their concerns

他們的擔憂是本於各自部門裡的競爭狀態　換言之
are based on the respective competitive dynamics within their departments. In other

他們擔心特別別引休假可能會使得本已經 (土) /ek'sæsə,bet/ = worsen =degenerate
words, they are worried that this special bonus might exacerbate an already highly

(土) 高度爭論和競爭的氣氛更加惡化　因此會打擾到他們想辦法維持到現在的
contentious and competitive atmosphere, thereby disturbing the uneasy equilibrium

相稱平衡狀態
they have managed to hold so far.

有個部門主管特別哀悼(哀叫)說獎勵的一週假(5天上班日), 在我們原本休假制度就很
2. One department head in particular has bemoaned the awarding of an extra

大方的時候
week (five working days) leave when our current leave policy is already generous,

可能太大方況了. 他的個人意見是這樣的　所以用更申一次, 以日話及來說
perhaps too generous in this individual's opinion. So again, in plain terms, this

這個人覺得我們部門已經被缺席滿搞得很緊繃了　n. 缺勤, 缺滿
individual feels that our departments are already strained by absenteeism and

還有固定假日, 而一個人有假超過一週會讓事迹況更糟
regular vacations, and that one more person out for one more week just makes

關於這點我想要特別說一下. 如果, 這項疑慮要被提出來的話, 我在會議 (184)
things worse. I would like to note that on this point, I strongly disagree and plan

上會提出我的強烈不同意 (主管嫌假多員工不可能嫌)
on saying so at the meeting, should this concern be raised.

If this concern should be raised

(185) 也許關於政策的措辭在會議中會被澄清, 我們全部都同意我們被這個措辭混了
3. Perhaps the wording of the policy will be cleared up in the meeting but all of

us agree that we are confused by the sentence: "The bonus leave will be accounted

for separately and will remain available until used, notwithstanding any other

limitation of annual leave that may be carried forward." Exactly what does that
繼續存在
mean? The leave can be carried over or it cannot be carried over? The habit carries over from his
這句到底是什麼意思? 這個假可以繼續存在還是不行?　childhood.

Thanks for your time and I look forward to discussing these issues with you.
謝您在時間並期待能進一步和您討論這些疑慮　習慣地從小保持至今

Yours,

Pete

*contentious　*strain　*exacerbate　v. 使惡化
adj. 愛爭論的, 有爭議的　v. 拉緊, 濫用　/ek'sæsə,bet/　使加劇

GO ON TO THE NEXT PAGE. →

181. Why did Deborah Lynn send the memo? memorandum

B

通知 (A) To inform her employees of an
下 impending move. 通知員工有個即將到來的搬家
宣佈 (B) To announce a policy change. 宣佈政策改變
(C) To ask for volunteers 徵求自願者
(D) To explain a new rule. 解釋一項新規定

→ explanation n 說明. 解釋

182. What will happen at the December 15 獎勵表現良好
meeting? 員工的這個

C

概念.
(A) They will discuss the annual
預算 budget. 會討論年度預算
(B) They will review current sick leave
policies. 會審查目前的病假政策
(C) They will select the employees
有~資格 eligible for the bonus. 會選出有資格得到額外
(D) They will decide how much the 假期的員工
bonus will be. 他們會決定獎勵會有多少.
獎金. 紅利. 額外津貼. 特別補助

183. Why did Pete Sears send the e-mail?

D

(A) He was angry about the
announcement. 對於這項宣佈很生氣
(B) He was wondering why he didn't
get the memo. 他在想為何他沒有得到 memo
(C) He was happy to hear about the
policy change. 他很開心聽到政策改變
(D) He was chosen by his co-workers
to raise their concerns with
Deborah. 他被同事選出來把疑慮提給 Deborah.

184. What does Pete Sears strongly
disagree with? 他超級不同意什麼?

A

(A) The idea that the employees
already have enough vacation
time. 員工已經有足夠的休假時間了
(B) The concept of awarding bonuses
for outstanding performance. idea
(C) The method by which employees
are evaluated. 員工被評估的方法
(D) The manner in which Deborah
announced the change.
Deborah 宣佈這項改變的方法

185. Which of the following is NOT a
concern mentioned in Pete's e-mail?

D

(A) The bonus may upset the 獎勵會
employee dynamic. 降低員工動力
(B) The employees already get
enough leave. 員工已有足夠休假
(C) The wording of the policy change
is unclear. 政策改變的措辭不清楚
(D) The performance evaluations may
be flawed. 表現評估的方法有缺陷
↳ flawless
→ flaw n. 缺陷. 瑕疵
There's a flaw in your plan.
n. 一陣狂風
The old man could hardly stand
on his feet in the flaw.
老人在這陣狂風中幾乎站不住了

* impending adj. 即將發生的. 迫近的
The dark clouds suggest an impending storm.
烏雲表明暴風雨即將來臨.
He was inadequately prepared for the impending
examinations. 他對即將舉行的考試準備不足.

# dynamic n. 動力
紅之工 adj. 動力的. 動態的
有活力的 a dynamic young person

* wonder (V) 納悶. 想知道. 覺得奇怪
→ I wonder whether you like her. 我不知道你是否喜歡她
→ I wonder at her rudeness. 我對他的粗魯感到驚訝.
(n) 驚嘆. 驚奇: There was a look of wonder in his eyes.
眼神中露出驚奇的神色.

| From: | Franklin Steves (PPT U.S.) |
|-------|----------------------------|
| To:   | Carmen Garcia (PPT Ecuador) |
| Re:   | Delmonico Steel |
| Date: | May 10 |

Hello Franklin,

I understand that you are making arrangements for Delmonico Steel's visit from Ecuador in June. I wanted to let you know that we at the PPT Ecuador office have been providing ongoing services for Delmonico Steel's operations here in Quito for the past seven years. Now that they are establishing an office in Miami, they are eager to partner with PPT there as well. Reaching an agreement with them should be fairly straightforward.

Regarding the welcome reception you are planning for June, I am aware that several on Delmonico's negotiating team have very specific food preferences and needs. Please take this into consideration.

Let me know if I can help in any way.

Regards,

Carmen

為你下次慶祝活動的賓客選擇最好的.
# Choose <u>the very best</u> for your guests

高帽子外燴公司 for your next celebration.
提供超棒的服務和用餐                Celebrate v. 慶祝.
Top Hat Catering has been providing excellence
                          不論休閒或是正式場合的活動
in service and dining for both casual and formal
以下就是我們和別人  在Tampa已超過25年了    dining table 餐桌
不一樣的原因.      events in Tampa for over 25 years.  dining room 餐廳
                                        dashboard dining
Set... apart from 使某人/某事與眾不同或優於其他的   邊開車邊用餐

Here is what <u>sets</u> Top Hat Catering <u>apart from</u> its competitors:
我們可以照不同的飲食限制改意所有的菜單品項  adj. 飲食的    n. 飲食的規定
• We can <u>adapt</u> all menu items to different dietary restrictions.
        adv 使適應.使適合.改編改意.
• We can arrange live entertainment for your event.
↳ 我們可以為你的活動安排 現場娛樂活動
• We provide complete cleanup service after each event.
↳ 每場活動後我們提供完整的清理服務
• We cater events from 12:00 noon to 11:00 P.M., seven days a week,
  365 days a year. 我們全年無休提供 中午12:00到晚上11:00的外燴服務

  請撥打我們的預約熱線 預訂你的活動吧?
Call our <u>reservations</u> hotline at 305-749-1170 to book your event

now!  *adapt v.
    ① He tried hard to adapt himself to the new condition. 適應
    ② The author is going to adapt his play for television. 改意
    ③ The boys adapted the old barn for use by the club. 改建

*reserve
v. 儲備.保存 → These seats are reserved for special guests.
              We'll reserve the money, we may need it later.

  預約.預訂 → We have reserved rooms at a hotel.

  延遲作決 → The court will reserve judgement.

n. 儲備, (物)(金)(量)
  克制,謹言: He spoke with reserve. 他說話謹慎

38

# BISCAYNE HOTEL
## A WAVERLY INTERNATIONAL PROPERTY

June 8

Dear Mr. Caruso,

Welcome to Tampa. I trust your journey was a pleasant one. Our team would like to invite you and your team to a welcome reception at 7:00 tonight here in the Biscayne Hotel. It will be held in the Causeway Room on the hotel's third floor. Please join us for this dinner so we can get to know each other better in advance of our upcoming business meetings.

If you require any assistance, please contact me at 305-525-3250.

Sincerely,
Franklin Chou

---

186. What is the main purpose of the e-mail?
(A) To revise a client's itinerary.
(B) To review a contract.
(C) To coordinate with another office about a client.
(D) To update a meeting agenda.

187. What makes Top Hat Catering an appropriate vendor for the PPT event?
(A) Its flexible menu.
(B) Its affordability.
(C) Its entertainment options.
(D) Its selection of venues.

189. For what company does Mr. Caruso most likely work?
(A) PPT Ecuador.
(B) Delmonico Steel.
(C) Top Hat Catering.
(D) Waverly International.

188. Based on the information in the advertisement, what kind of event would Top Hat Catering be unlikely to cater?
(A) A holiday dinner.
(B) A birthday party.
(C) A business breakfast.
(D) A wedding reception.

190. When did Mr. Caruso most likely receive the note?
(A) When he checked into his hotel.
(B) When he finished a series of business meetings.
(C) When he arrived at PPT U.S.'s offices.
(D) When he landed at an airport.

*GO ON TO THE NEXT PAGE.*

39

*Valid adj. 有根據的. 令人信服的. 合法的. 有效的. 經正當手續的
→ His arguement is valid. 她的論點站得住腳
→ It's a valid contract. 有法律效力的合同
→ The ticket is valid for one month. 這票一個月內有效.

×estimate
(n.) 估價. 估計. 評斷. 看法
→ My estimate of the situation is not so optimistic. 我對形勢的估計沒那麼樂觀

(V.) 估計. 估價 I asked a contractor to estimate for the repair of the house.
請承包商估價這棟房子的費用

## GOLDSBORO LOGISTICS

| Relocation Packages | Schedule a Visit | Insurance | FAQ |

選擇一個最適合的搬家方案. 然後按下 "安排拜訪" 鈕. 安排到府估價
Choose the relocation package that best suits your needs, then click the
"Schedule a Visit" tab to arrange an in-house estimate. Each relocation
(帽子的)護耳.(易開罐的)拉環. 本公上提供時間的標
relocate
package comes with an optional storage-space lease plan (SSLP). The SSLP
(上)
fees listed are valid until 30 June. 每一個搬家方案都有一個可買可不買的儲存空間租用
可選. 清單上的價格有效到6/30. 包含搬家卡車和團隊至高到4小時. 捆帶. 捆尺.

標準 Standard: Includes moving truck and crew for up to four hours, ropes and
straps, and two handcarts. SSLP fee: $50 first month; $65 every month
thereafter. 2台手推車. 空間租用價格: 第-個月50, 之後每個月65

包含標準方案的所有特色. 再加上盒子. 箱子及藝術品. 盤子. 電視. 電腦設備
高 Superior: Includes all features of the standard package plus boxes and
級 covers for artwork, dishes, TVs, computer accessories, and mattresses.
地毯等的外罩防護
SSLP fee: $60 first month; $75 every month thereafter.
第-個月60. 之後每個月75 / 包含所有高級方案有的再加上打包和做記號

豪 Deluxe: Includes all features of the superior package plus packing and
華 /dɪˈlʌks/
labeling of boxes (content and room location). SSLP fee: $70 first month;
$85 every month thereafter. (內容物及房間, 第-個月70. 之後每個月85    真空

包含豪華方案所有. 再加上吸房間和地毯汙漬. 清除 *vacuum v. 吸 n. 真空
高 Premium: Includes all features of the deluxe package plus vacuuming of (10電的)
端 (下)
豪 rooms and removal of carpet stains. SSLP fee: $80 first month; $95 every
華 month thereafter. 第-個月80. 之後每個月95    他同意搬走旗幟
→ n. 移動. 搬遷. 排除. 清除 → He consented to the removal of the flags.

*Stain v. 沾汙 Blood stained the blanket.
/e/
沾汙 His crimes stained the family honor. 他的罪敗壞了家庭名譽
給(木材. 玻璃著色) She stained the table brown.
n. 汙點. 瑕疵 His character is without stain. 人品純潔無瑕.

| From: | Dave Goldsboro |
| To: | Karen Meeks |
| Re: | Your Move: First Stage Complete |
| Date: | May 1 |

*transport  *The goods will be transported to Tokyo*

(v) 運輸, 運送, 搬運  *The van isn't big enough by air.*

*to transport my furniture.*

(n) 運輸, 交通工具, 狂喜  ↳ 這輛貨車不夠大, 運不了我的傢俱

→ *The machines are ready for transport.*  *She was in a transport of delight*
機器待運  *at the good news.* 她聽到這好消息欣喜若狂。

Dear Ms. Meeks,

這封信是告訴您, 您的東西已被移到從359到我們的儲存單位放置了

This is to let you know that your <u>belongings</u> have now been transported 設備

from 359 Plainfield Rd. in Woodridge to our <u>storage</u> <u>facility</u> in Downers 場所 地點 廁所

Grove and placed in a <u>storage unit</u>. Per the terms of your SSLP, they

特要在最後放在這裡直到5/31   權據您存放的條款   到那時東西會被平移到你的新家

will <u>remain</u> here until May 31, at which time they will be <u>transferred</u> to

your new home at 109 Fairfield Rd., Downers Grove.   A→B | carry

若您希望延長儲存時間超過目前的結束時間, 您一定要在動了天前通知我們你的

If you wish to <u>extend</u> your SSLP <u>beyond</u> the current end date of May   決定

out   ↳ 遲於, 晚於, 在~的另一邊

31, you must <u>notify</u> us of your decision at least three (3) days <u>in</u>

<u>advance</u>. Moreover, for every month that your belongings are stored

→ 房產部轄全經營場所   費用如您所租用方案指明的

on our <u>premises</u> beyond May 31, a fee as <u>specified</u> in your SSLP will

/premisiz/   specify v 指明, 具體說明

be <u>automatically charged to your account</u> on the first day of every

month.   會自動地記到您的帳上, 每個月1號的時候。 → The directions specify how

the medicine is to be used. 說明書上明確

若您有任何問題, 請聯繫我們。

If you have any questions, please do not <u>hesitate</u> to contact us. 指明這藥如何使用

/hezɪtet/

*I'd like to set up automatic bill payment for my utility bills.*
我想把我的水電瓦斯帳單設定為自動扣款

Best regards,

Dave Goldsboro   *Does this bank offer an automatic bill payment service?*

Goldsboro Logistics   這間銀行有提供自動扣繳服務嗎?

*notify v 通知, 報告  → *He notified the police of the incident.*

/notə,faɪ/ 告知, 宣佈   *The sale was notified in the newspapers.* 刊登報上

*transfer (v) 轉換, 調動, 轉印

*She has been transferred to another department.*   幾乎時間他們就把荒地變成

*Her father transferred her to a better school.* ↗   良田

*Within a few years they had transferred barren waste into fertile fields.*

transfer (n) 移交, 調任, 轉讓者, 過戶, 過戶憑單, 匯錢   * /fɜtl/ adj. 多產的, 肥沃的

*He wants a transfer to another team.* 銀行支票匯錢   他想像力豐富 繁殖力強的

*The transfer of money by bank check is very common today.*   *He's fertile of imagination.*

GO ON TO THE NEXT PAGE. ➡

41

| From: | Karen Meeks |
| To: | Dave Goldsboro /'kɔːldzbɔːI/ |
| Re: | Your Move: First Stage Complete |
| Date: | May 2 |

\* courtesy n. 禮貌. 殷勤. 好意
He wrote back to her out of courtesy.
他出於禮貌給她寫了一封回信.

\* thoroughness n. 徹底. 完全　總裁對於他辦事有效率又極認真佔細
The president was impressed by his speed and thoroughness. 印象深刻。

Dear Mr. Goldsboro,

謝謝您的來信. 我很感謝您的好意. 專業. 和您團隊的徹底(認真佔細)
Thank you for your e-mail. I was very impressed with the courtesy (UP)
/əˈsɔːnɪs/　每一個房間
professionalism, and thoroughness of your crew. Each room, the
包括地下室　　　都是乾淨的　　　連墨水漬. 之前在我工作房地毯上的
basement included, was perfectly clean. Even an ink stain that was
on the carpet in my home office is now hardly visible. 都幾乎看不到了.

請注意. 由於預料之外的情況. 我們搬進去的日期改變了
Please note that due to unforeseen circumstances, our move-in date
has changed. We now need our items to be transferred to 109
Fairfield Road on Friday, June 7. 我們需要在6/7 週五時把東西搬去 Fairfield 路
　最後, 我們想確認您的儲存空間是溫控的
Finally, we would like to confirm that your storage units are
　　　　　我們很擔心我們的古董桌有可能受損.
climate-controlled. We are worried that an antique table of ours might
be ruined if exposed to excessive heat or humidity. antique adj. 古代的
如果暴露在過熱或者過潮溼的環境下. /ænˈtiːk/　　古老的

Sincerely,
↳ \* ruin　　　　　　　　　　　　　　　n. 古董
Karen Meeks
(V) 使毀滅. 毀壞 The heavy rain ruined our holiday.
　　　　　The typhoon ruined all the houses here.

(n) 毀滅. 廢墟. 禍因 → Drink was his father's ruin and it will be the ruin
↳ We visited the ruins of the temple.　　　of him too.

\* unforeseen → The circumstances were totally unforeseen.
adj. 未預見的　　This turn of fortune was unforeseen.
　預料之外的　　　　這時來的轉變是沒有預料到的.

\* expose
out | put
① 曝光: Don't expose the film to light.
② 揭露: Their scheme was exposed.
③ 使曝露於: They consider it almost a crime
　　　　　to expose children to violence and sex on TV.

42

191. According to the webpage, what is true about Goldsboro's storage-space lease plans? 在到府估價拜訪之前要先付錢
根據網頁 闡述此句意何者為真?
C
(A) They must be paid for before a home visit is arranged. 只在有限時間內有效
(B) They are available for a limited time.
(C) Their rates vary by relocation package. 因搬家方案不同,收費不同
(D) Their rates change every three months. 費率每三個月更改一次

⊘ 修改.變更 使不同. Teachers should vary their lessons.
老師應讓課多樣化.

192. According to the second e-mail, what is Ms. Meeks concerned about? 根據第二封e-mail,他擔憂付麼?
C
(A) A spot on her carpet. 地毯上的點點
(B) The size of her storage unit 儲存單位的大小
(C) Damage to her furniture. 傢俱受損
(D) The loss of her copy of the SSLP contract. 失去,用去合約複本

損失.減少.失敗.喪失→ He suffered a temporary loss of memory. 暫時喪失記憶

193. What is the purpose of the first e-mail? 告知一個服務的狀態
A
(A) To report on the status of a service.
(B) To request payment. 要求付款
(C) To answer a customer's question. 回答客人的問題
(D) To communicate an invoicing error. 溝通一則發票失誤
invoice

194. What service package did Ms. Meeks most likely choose? 他最有可能是選擇
D
(A) Standard. 哪一種方案呢?
(B) Superior. ＊request v.n. 要求
(C) Deluxe. They requested financial
(D) Premium. all my requests 　support.
關於他的敘述何者為真? were granted.

195. What is implied about Goldsboro Logistics? 不能符合他的要求
(A) It cannot meet Ms. Meeks's request. 6/1開始要多收他錢
(B) It will charge Ms. Meeks an additional fee on June 1.
(C) Its Woodridge facility will be relocating to Downers Grove
relocate
(D) Its crew has often been praised for its professionalism. —ism
員工們時常因為專業程度受到誇獎. 表行為
學說.特性
journalism 新聞業
communism 共產主義
capitalism 資本主義
optimism 樂觀主義
pessimism 悲觀主義

＊國外invoice → is a request for payment → 給你看要付的詳細清單
receipt → is a proof of payment → 證明你已付過錢
但現在不太分.因為通常一張上面會有這兩種資訊.
台灣可以對統一號碼的 → Treasury Invoice 財政部發票
VAT Invoice (Value-added Tax) 商業稅發票
uniform Invoice 統一發票
→ There are 17 NTD 10 million jackpot winners for the Taiwan receipt lottery
in November 2018. 統一發票得獎. 台灣才有的收據式彩透

＊praise n. 讚揚.稱讚 I'm sure he doesn't deserve so much praise.
/preɪz/ v. 讚美.表揚 The mayor praised the boy for his courage.
The publishers praised his novel pretty highly.
出版商們對他的小說評價甚高.

GO ON TO THE NEXT PAGE.

*enable v. 賦予…能力 = Training will enable you to find work.
使成為可能 = The program will enable a large increase in students numbers.

# LA Phil
CENTENNIAL CAMPAIGN 100

# Support LA PHIL

p 就是使世界級的音樂表演已經要邁入第100年了
**The Los Angeles Philharmonic** is entering its 100th year of
presenting world-class musical performances. Please help us continue
請幫助我們持續這項傳統
this tradition by becoming a Philharmonic sponsor. Your financial
藉由變成我們的贊助者                            你的財務支持
support will enable us to maintain low ticket prices and keep our music
(v.)
accessible to everyone.  讓我們能夠保持低票價並且讓每個人都能接觸我們
                                                                的音樂
你會收到很多特別的好處來交換您的財務捐款
You receive many special benefits in exchange for your financial
donation. The list below shows the benefits offered at each level of
support.  下面這張清單秀出每種等級的支持能得到的好處

收到我們的音樂CD          /'peɪtrən/ n. 贊助者  We have a special offer
和一年份的音樂雜誌 一般捐    讓願     for our regular patrons.
**Patron Sponsor** ($100 - $399): 我們給老顧客特別的優惠
Receive the music CD *The Delightful Sounds of the Los Angeles
Philharmonic* and a one-year subscription to *California Music* subscribe
*Spotlight* (published six times annually). 一年出版6次  訂閱 under I write
                                           v. 認捐, 在文件下面簽名
除了一般捐的好處外    季捐
另加上所有票打85折  **Season Sponsor** ($400 - $999): They subscribed to local
                                           charities. 向當地團體捐款
Receive *The Delightful Sounds of the Los Angeles Philharmonic*,
a one-year subscription to *California Music Spotlight* and a 15%
discount on all LA PHIL concert tickets.  → Each of us subscribed for 500
                                           我們個人認購500股  shares.
除了上述好處外,      大手筆捐→傑作
可以特別預約坐位 **Masterworks Sponsor** ($1000 or more):
    Receive Season Sponsor benefits, special reserved seating, and
    the opportunity to dine with the Philharmonic conductor James
    Colby-Ross at LA PHIL's annual musicians' dinner. 有機會和指揮 James
              在 LA Phil's 年度音樂晚享上用饗。
請把你的捐款寄至
Please send your donation to: Support LA PHIL, 801 S. 7th Street, Los
Angeles, CA 90021. To learn about more ways to support the Los
Angeles Philharmonic, please call our support coordinator Jennifer
                                           coordinate adj. 同等的
Carmichael at 323-545-2813, or write to her at the address above.
                                           同等重要的
想知道更多支持我們的方法,請致電我們贊助活動主辦人 Jennifer
                                           n. 同等的人
或是寄信到上述地址給她.  Citizens are coordinates in a court of law.
                        公民在法庭上是平等的。

44

# LA Phil 100
CENTENNIAL CAMPAIGN

## Southern California Times Masterworks

100週年活動，我們不能缺了您一塊來慶祝。

It's the 100th anniversary of The Los Angeles Philharmonic.  We can't
celebrate without you!  *pull out all the stops: to do everything you can to make something*
*successful*

音樂指揮MC 使出渾身解數為了重要的 南加洲時代傑作系列

Music Director Michael Cavaleri is pulling out all the stops for our premier
*adj. 首位的 / 較早的 / 最早的*
*歷史*

Southern California Times Masterworks series, with some of the most
用了一些最高要求的作品展示你們的音樂大師陳列，展示
/ˈvɜːtʃuˈoʊsoʊ/

demanding masterpieces in history to showcase your virtuoso Los Angeles
在L.A., San Diego 和 Santa Barbara 都有音樂會

Philharmonic.  With concerts in L.A., San Diego, and Santa Barbara, the
南加洲時代傑作系列可以買 14.10.7.5場
請我們新的 matinée 系列，在Wiltern劇院

Southern California Times Masterworks series is available in packages of,
身為訂購者
x&e

14, 10, 7 and 5 concerts, including our new matinée series at the Wiltern
你得到用上優質票價 30.45 可以買 top 全到的位子.

Theater.  As a subscriber, you receive premium seating at the same low
ticket prices for the top tier $30 and $45 seats at each concert.

訂購者持續享有免費的彈性票券更換，免費的朋友券、多買票打9折

Subscribers continue to enjoy free flexible ticket exchanges, free friend
還有

vouchers, a 10% discount on additional ticket purchases, and advance
特別演出的最好坐位資訊能優先得到          按優例分佈的方案現在可以買了

notice for best seats to our concert specials.  Pro-rated packages are now
電下單訂購、按下連結各鍵          (不用一次買完我買後場買幾場

available.  To order your subscription, click the series links below to
來線上購買或者致電

purchase online or call the LA PHIL Ticket Center at 727.892.3337 or
周一到周五

1.800.662.7286 Monday through Friday, 9:00 AM to 5:00 PM, or Saturday
and Sunday, 10:00 AM to 3:00 PM.  You can also contact the Ticket Center
by e-mail at ticketcenter@laphil.org. 也可以用e-mail 和訂票中心聯絡

For a PDF version of the Masterworks series, click here.  For a PDF
version of the series break out, click here.

a series          發生          stage
ni 專績、系列)          left          舞台          right
                         box          orchestra          box
a series of attacks 一串的攻擊          管弦樂隊
     measures 系列的措施          grand tier — lodge

upper
lower  > balcony

GO ON TO THE NEXT PAGE.

45

| Masterworks Pricing | Walt Disney Concert Hall | Wiltern Theater | Ruth Eckerd Hall |
|---|---|---|---|
| Imperial (14 concerts) $420 - $630 | Click to buy | Click to buy | not available |
| Intermezzo (10 concerts) $450 - $300 | Click to buy | Click to buy | Click to buy |
| Fanfare (7 concerts) $315 - $210 | not available | not available | not available |
| Ovation (7 concerts) $315 - $210 | Click to buy | Click to buy | Click to buy |
| Matinees (5 concerts) $225 - $150 | Click to buy | Click to buy | not available |

*Imperial* adj. 帝國的 最高的, 特優的. 宏大的
→ Uncle is well known for his imperial generosity. 叔父的寬宏大量是出了名的。

*Intermezzo* n. 插曲, 間奏曲

in a fanfare of publicity 大張旗鼓地
n. 儀式開始前的喇叭聲, 誇耀, 炫耀

→ The hero received a great ovation from the crowd. 受到群眾熱烈歡迎
*ovation* n. 熱烈歡迎, 鼓掌 → The show won a standing ovation. 起立鼓掌

*Matinees* 日戲, 日場

* solicit v. 懇求, 徵求
→ They are busy soliciting votes. 他們正忙著拉選票。
廣告的主旨為何? → to solicit sth. from sb. 向某人索要某物
他在 LA Phil 的職位是什麼?

**196.** What is the main purpose of the advertisement? 要求捐款
(A) To solicit donations. 懇請
(B) To announce a new schedule. 宣佈新行程
(C) To introduce a new musician. 介紹新的音樂家
(D) To promote an upcoming festival. 宣傳即將到來的慶典
v. 晉升·促進, 宣傳, 引起

**199.** What is Michael Cavaleri's role with the LA Phil?
(A) Conductor. 指揮（籌辦活動的人）
(B) Support coordinator. 協調支持人
(C) Music director. 音樂總監
(D) Magazine publisher. 雜誌出版人員

**197.** What is indicated about The Los Angeles Philharmonic?
(A) It is moving to a new location. 搬到新地點
(B) It is celebrating a milestone. 慶祝一個里程碑
(C) It is funded by local taxes. 用當地稅收資助
(D) It is a for-profit corporation. 是個營利公司 ↔ not-for-profit 的

**200.** Which Masterworks series is completely sold out? 哪一個系列已完全賣完了
(A) Imperial. 特優方案
(B) Intermezzo. 間奏曲方案
(C) Fanfare. 開場方案（粉絲方案）
(D) Ovation. 鼓掌方案

**198.** According to the website, what is new at the Wiltern Theater?
(A) A matinée series. 有日場系列
(B) Premium seating. 有高級坐位
(C) Friend vouchers. 有好友券
(D) Ticket exchanges. 有票券交換

* premium (adj) 優質的, 高價的  premium vodka
① 獎品, 獎金
額外補貼. 津貼
附贈禮品: If you buy three you get a premium of one more, free.
加價: Hard-to-get theater tickets can be bought at a premium. 難買的票可以用高價買到
gift 票券
a luncheon voucher discount

Stop!  This is the end of the test.  If you finish before time is called, you may go back to Parts 5, 6, and 7 and check your work.

心得筆記欄

# 新制多益全眞模擬試題⑭教師手冊
New Format
TOEIC Model Test

售價：150 元

主　　　編／劉　毅
發　行　所／學習出版有限公司　　　　☎ (02) 2704-5525
郵 撥 帳 號／05127272 學習出版社帳戶
登　記　證／局版台業 2179 號
印　刷　所／裕強彩色印刷有限公司
台 北 門 市／台北市許昌街 17 號 6F　　☎ (02) 2331-4060
台灣總經銷／紅螞蟻圖書有限公司　　　☎ (02) 2795-3656
本公司網址／www.learnbook.com.tw
電 子 郵 件／learnbook@learnbook.com.tw

2021 年 8 月 1 日初版

ISBN 978-986-231-462-3

版權所有，本書內容未經書面同意，不得以任何
形式複製。